SINFUL MAFIA SANTA

SINFUL MAFIA SANTA

A DIAMOND RING DARK ROMANCE

THE SINFUL MAFIA SERIES

ALIX KEY

DIAMOND
FREEPORT PRESS

Published by Diamond Freeport Press
P.O. Box 42133, Arlington, VA 22204

ISBN 978-1-95018-494-1

Discover other titles by Alix Key at www.alixkey.com

101625ak

ALSO BY ALIX KEY

Find a complete, up-to-date list of Alix's books at www.alixkey.com.

The Kidnapped Series

Diamond Solitaire

Rough Diamond

Conflict Diamond

Priceless Diamond

The Irish Mob Trilogy

Irish Brute

Irish Vice

Irish Reign

The Boston Mob Trilogy

Her Irish Savage

Her Irish Protector

Her Irish King

The Taming the Mob Princess Trilogy

Taken Enemy

Twisted Enemy

Tamed Enemy

The Sinful Mafia Series

Sinful Mafia Santa

Sinful Mafia Deception

Sinful Mafia Seduction

Sinful Mafia Salvation

WORD OF WARNING

***Sinful Mafia Santa* is a dark romance.**

It contains hard-to-read scenes, graphic language, and explicit sexual content.

A complete list of potential triggers can be found at:

https://alixkey.com/books/sinful-mafia-series/

Please don't read this book if you are sensitive to any of those triggers. But if you believe in the power of true love to bring joy and fulfillment to consenting adults, then this is the book for you.

Welcome to the Diamond Ring.

1

AERYN

There are two kinds of people who go to an underground sex club the week before Christmas: The lonely and the curious.

Wait. There's a third kind too: Chefs who need to blow off a little steam after furiously plating orders for the last seating on a busy Friday, four nights before the holiday.

"I'm absolutely knackered," I say, the Irish coming out in my voice as I collapse into a chair in Will Lasker's cluttered office. "And all *I* had to do was shove mixed greens onto plates."

"Bullshit," Will says, sucking deep on his vape pen. "You are a *goddess*, Aeryn Reardon. You took over that salad station like you've worked here all your life. And you didn't even break a sweat."

Well, I *did* strip down to my black silk shell—Miu Miu for the win. My Alexander McQueen cardigan is draped over the back of my chair. My matching high-waist trousers are no worse for wear, but I traded in my Louboutin heels for a spare pair of Will's Crocs.

It's been eight years since Will and I completed our coursework at the New York Culinary Institute. Even when Will was smoking cigarettes instead of vaping, he could taste the difference between orange and yellow bell peppers, blindfolded. Now, the salads he serves at Nourriture are works of art.

"Are you going to fire that shitehawk?" The man I stood in for showed up an hour late, higher than the Empire State Building.

"I already did," Will says. "Want a full-time job?"

I laugh. "You can't afford me. Besides, I have to be back in Chicago by Christmas Day."

"Want a three-day job?" Will persists. He waggles his eyebrows at me. "I'll make it worth your while."

I laugh. "And how will you do that?"

"Come on," he says, pushing back from his desk. "I'll take you to Kynk."

I snort. "You and I parted ways with *kink* the night you decided to fuck Jaxon Pearson in the classroom walk-in."

"Kynk," he says again, and he spells it. He doesn't bother apologizing for Jaxon. Will and I are much better friends than we ever were lovers. And part of me always knew he preferred boys, even when we were dating.

"Sorry," I say. "I don't think *Kynk* made it onto TripAdvisor's list of Top Ten New York Attractions."

"There's a reason for that," Will says. "It's the most exclusive sex club in all five boroughs."

"But they let you in," I point out.

"*I* am a card-carrying member."

"So not so exclusive then."

"Do I need to remind you that I am the owner and chef de cuisine of the restaurant *The New York Times* called 'First in Class' last year?"

Will doesn't need to remind me. I'm still green with envy—

greener than the kale microgreens I tweezed onto his salads for the last four hours. He's living his dream here in Manhattan, while I'm stuck back in Chicago.

My week-long vacation to New York has been one last hurrah before I accept the inevitable and take my place in the Reardon family business. An obedient daughter, I've given notice at the Chicago Art Institute, telling them they need a new chef for their museum café.

It was never a Michelin-starred restaurant like Will's, but it was a job I got on my own merit. I'll miss it. A lot. I'll never be as happy, fulfilling my obligations as to Chicago's Irish mob.

"Hey," Will croons, as if he realizes he touched a live nerve. "We don't have to go."

I force myself to laugh. "Friday night at a sex club in New York City with my gay ex-boyfriend? How can I possibly say no?"

"Have you been to one before?"

"What? You think Chicago is the boonies?"

"I thought maybe—"

"I've been to a feckin' club."

I don't tell him it was three rooms in the dank basement of a Chicago brownstone. That I went with three girlfriends from high school, when we all decided to skip our tenth reunion at St. Boniface. That I had a couple of drinks, walked around in lingerie bought for the purpose, and decided I would never understand the appeal of butt plugs with animal tails attached. I was home, alone, asleep in my own bed by midnight—and that was *after* a session with my favorite hot pink vibrator.

Will is already on his feet, bouncing like arborio rice spilled onto a linoleum floor. I swear to God the man must be vaping pure adrenaline. "Let's go, then!" He sniffs at his chef's jacket. "Jesus. I reek. Thank God Kynk has showers."

"Thank God," I drawl.

I barely have time to switch out my shoes and pull on my sweater before he's hustling me out the door. I'm still knotting the belt on my sturdy winter overcoat when a cab glides to the curb in response to his raised hand.

I gaze out the windows as we make our way down Fifth Avenue. The city is decorated for Christmas, brilliantly colored lights reflecting off the fresh snow that fell during dinner service. Even though it's late, there are still lots of people on the pavement, gawking at brightly lit store windows.

Will ignores the holiday finery. Instead, he fills me in on the menu he's launching next month, twenty-one all-new courses. I make appropriate noises at all the right places, but by the time Will gets to his three desserts—each one-bite morsel more elaborate than the last—I finally interrupt. "Wait. Where *is* this club we're going to?"

"Brooklyn," he says, waving toward the bridge we're about to cross.

I sigh. I wanted to avoid Brooklyn this trip. I wanted to steer clear of the memories.

"Down by the waterfront," Will adds.

That's even worse.

Will leans forward, concern carving lines between his eyebrows. He's right. He reeks. "Change your mind?" he asks.

"No," I say too quickly, shaking my head. "It's just that…"

Will waits at least thirty seconds before he prompts, "Just that…"

I sigh. "Logan was going to open a club in Brooklyn."

Will's eyes go wide with horror-tinged pity. Or maybe that's pity-tinged horror. I know both looks well.

I despise being Logan Reardon's little sister. Even people who've never watched a minute of professional hockey have seen footage of my brother sprawled on the ice at Aces Arena, his arterial blood neon-red against the blue crease in front of the goal.

Logan died ten years ago Christmas Eve. It was a freak accident. A fight, like a dozen other line brawls across the league that night. Logan just happened to fall as another player's skate came up. One inch to the left or the right and he would have taken a stitch or two, been back on the ice before the end of the period. Instead, his carotid was dissected and he bled out in three minutes flat, in front of eighteen thousand fans. In the past decade, millions have watched the replay on social media.

Will finally whispers, his voice low with respect, "Logan planned to open a sex club?"

My laugh sounds shaky. I doubt my straitlaced brother ever said the word *fetish* in his life, much less indulged in one. He was always an athlete, always in training.

Of course, growing up a Reardon, Logan knew his way around underground establishments. On his eighteenth birthday, he made his vows to the South Side Squad, taking his place in our Irish mob clan beside my da and our four older brothers.

But Logan's future was always on the ice rink. Not in strip clubs and after-hours bars, not liberating "lost" trailers in night raids at Chicago's trucking terminal, not stepping into some sweetheart job at Reardon Construction.

I tell Will, "He wanted to set up a sports bar in one of those abandoned subway tunnels. He was going into business with one of his teammates. They planned on getting athletes to drop by on the regular, keep the crowds coming, you know? I was going to do the food—wagyu sliders, heritage pork bratwurst, international beers, that sort of thing."

"I'm sorry it didn't happen." Will sounds sincere.

"I am too." I was frozen for nearly a year after Logan died, unable to accept that he was gone, unable to go back to culinary school, unable to do just about anything but haunt the Reardon family mansion in Chicago.

I'm Da's only daughter. He indulged me. He always has.

Until now.

Da has given me one year to get married, and he's pushing me hard toward one of the old Irish families. The only restaurant he'll tolerate my running is a manky diner on the South Side, a place to launder his mob money. He's already picked out the location, promising to burn out the existing restaurant if the current owner doesn't sign over the lease by New Year's.

I'm lucky Da let me come to New York, let me say goodbye to the life I could have led. I've had one solid week of reservations at the city's finest dining establishments, but every meal rubs salt in my wounds. Korean amethyst bamboo salt, yeah, but salt all the same.

My dreams will die Tuesday morning, when I climb into Da's private jet and head back to Chicago for Christmas dinner with my clan. Once I set foot back on Squad territory, I'll be a good little Reardon girl for the rest of my feckin' life.

"Look," Will says. "If this is a bad night for you…"

"William Lasker, that's the third time you've asked if I'm having second thoughts. It sounds like *you're* the one thinking I shouldn't go to this club!"

"No way, Ariel." He's called me that since the first day of classes, when my red-brown hair refused to stay put in a respectable ponytail. He said I looked like the Little Mermaid, and I told him I looked better in a seashell bra than any animated character. After that, our friendship was sealed.

The cab pulls over to the curb in the middle of a block that looks condemned, and Will taps his credit card to pay. When we climb out of the car, I realize the snow has been cleared from a narrow section of sidewalk. We make our way to a shadowed door.

A discreet brass plaque engraved with the name—KYNK—is the only sign we've reached our destination. The hinges on the door look like they should squeal, but they swing open with velvet silence. We step into a foyer that resembles a trendy hotel for superstars, complete with two massive, tuxedoed security guards just inside the door.

"Good evening, Mr. Lasker," says a woman from behind a mahogany desk. Despite the fact that it's after midnight, she wears flawless makeup and a welcoming smile. A sprig of holly is fastened to one of the lapels of her burgundy suit. On the other, she wears four pins—a replica of the brass oval from the front door along with three flags: the United Arab Emirates, Japan, and Germany.

"Hey, Lydia," Will says. "This is my friend, Aeryn Reardon. She'll be joining me this evening."

Lydia doesn't seem to notice that Will smells like a fry cook. Nor does she react to the fact that I'm a woman—hardly Will's typical guest, I'm willing to bet. Instead, she gives me a professional smile. "It's a pleasure, Ms. Reardon. Have you played with us before?"

I catch myself smiling back, at maybe half the wattage. "I haven't had the opportunity."

"Well, welcome to Kynk." She waves a manicured hand toward a pair of polished wooden doors. "We invite you to step into our greenroom—ladies to your right. Inside, you'll find lockers for your convenience. We ask guests to undress to whatever level makes them feel most comfortable."

I nod. With the bouncers at this place looking like they could take down the entire Chicago Bears defensive line, I'll certainly feel comfortable taking off my black wool coat.

Lydia says, "We do require all our guests to leave behind any devices that capture audio or video, including cell phones."

That's another point in the club's favor. I decide I can shed my bouclé cardigan as well.

Lydia continues with her welcome pitch: "A door at the far end of the greenroom will take you to the club proper, by way of a metal detector."

There goes my silk shell. This is clearly a club that puts an emphasis on members' safety. My black lace lingerie is about to get a viewing. And I thought I only wore it as armor against jealousy, when I dressed for an evening at Will's elite restaurant.

"Once you're in the Great Room, I'm sure Mr. Lasker will show you around. We expect all our guests to determine their own safewords. Our security staff is present to protect you and all other guests. Please don't hesitate to ask for any assistance you require."

Will is nodding like he's listening to a favorite song, and I wonder how many times he's heard this welcoming spiel. I thank Lydia, and we take a couple of steps closer to the greenroom doors.

"I'm going to take a quick shower," Will says. "Meet you by the main bar in twenty?"

Yes, Chef, I start to say, the way I answered all his questions during dinner service. I catch myself in time and say, "Sounds good."

"Let's have a codeword," he says. "For when you want to leave."

"Who says I'll want to leave first?"

He grins. "For when *I* want to leave, then. How about *tiramisu?*"

"Tiramisu," I say. "Got it."

"Aren't *you* eager to get out on the floor?" he teases. Then: "Twenty minutes." He kisses me on the cheek, and I head into the women's greenroom.

The dressing room at that Chicago brownstone was a closet with a pull-string for a bare lightbulb overhead. Kynk's greenroom is a study in soft neutrals, gray and beige that have been kissed by lavender and peach. The air smells faintly of nutmeg and clove. A long mirror stretches to my right, reflecting a row of gleaming wooden lockers, each one decorated for the season with a large red bow. Through an alcove, I can glimpse private dressing rooms.

Two women take time from their whispered gossip by the mirror to smile distractedly at me. I can hear a shower running in the distance. Everything is peaceful. Calm.

Except the pounding of my heart.

I shake my head when I recognize the little flutter in my belly. It's been nearly six months since I broke up with Shea, Da's most recent candidate for a mob match. Although I've gone through half a dozen batteries in my vibrator, I haven't exactly been longing for male attention.

I'm half a continent away from home, from all the expectations that come with being Mickey Reardon's only daughter. Will is going to find a pretty boy to play with. And I just realized how much I want to do the same.

There. Decision made. I'm entering the Great Room in my knickers, my bra, and my red-soled stilettos.

I take a few minutes in front of the mirror. My hair is as hopeless as ever; I run my fingers through it, braid it loosely, take out the braid, and toss my head like a wild mustang. I have better luck with eye-liner—quick, decisive strokes to emphasize my dark green eyes. I add a dash of lipstick, drawing attention from my freckles.

I could spend more time in front of the mirror, but there isn't any point. I want to be out in the club.

Stepping through the metal detector, I take a moment to get my bearings. The room is long, its exposed brick walls curving into the distance. Black leather chairs and couches are arranged in convenient clusters, as if to encourage conversation.

There are more people than I expected, but it *is* a Friday night. Women are dressed in everything from full-body vinyl catsuits to bare skin. One man kneels nearby in a gimp suit, bowing his head in front of his leather-clad dominatrix. Other men wear trousers, or boxers, or nothing.

There's a surprising number of Santa hats in the crowd, and more than a few headbands with reindeer antlers. After I see my first-ever Prince Albert with a jingle bell attached, I realize I won't think of Father Christmas in quite the same way, ever again.

As I walk toward the main bar, some men eye me from comfortable seats. Two raise glasses in easy-to-ignore invitations. One woman mouths from her couch: "Great shoes!"

A couple orders drinks in front of me. He says he wants a Dewars on the rocks, but she contradicts before the bartender can pour. "Not tonight, Johnny. You've been a very bad boy. And what does Mommy say bad boys drink?"

"Milk," Johnny says, scowling.

"Johnny will have milk," Mommy says to the bartender.

The bartender pours cold milk into a highball glass with an apologetic smile to Johnny. I suspect the couple must be regulars.

The bartender turns to me. "And what can I get for you?"

"Whiskey," I say. "Neat."

He beams like I've aced my culinary school final on distilled spirits. "Do you have a preference?"

"She'll have the Jameson 18," says a man behind me.

I recognize the voice before I turn around. I've known it for years. I heard it the night Logan told me about his plans to open a sports bar with his best friend. I heard it the night I lost my v-card. The night my brother died.

"Aeryn," he says.

And I force myself to look into the eyes of Gage Rider.

2

GAGE

S he's stunning.

I haven't seen Aeryn Reardon since Logan's funeral, almost exactly ten years ago. Then, she was a twenty-one-year-old kid—angry at the world for the shit luck that took her brother in a freak accident. Angry with me for being on the ice when it happened, for being too concussed to try to stop the bleeding. Angry with me for a hell of a lot more, if I let myself remember the truth.

Now, she's a magnificent woman, with that mane of auburn hair and eyes as green as bottle glass. She's confident, with her shoulders back and her chin held high. She's distracting as hell in her high-end lingerie, wearing those red-soled shoes.

Aeryn always had good taste. Present company excepted.

I look straight into her eyes. "Of all the sex clubs in all the towns in all the world, you walk into mine."

"Gage," she says. Her voice is as cool as an ice rink as she accepts her pour of Jameson. Too late, I remember that Bogart loses Bacall in *Casablanca*.

I start to ask what brought her to New York, but I suspect her answer will be the upcoming anniversary. I have no idea how I'd respond to that, so I opt for a coward's escape instead. "Welcome to Kynk."

"Not quite the place you and Logan planned." So she isn't afraid to say his name.

"Plans changed." I gesture at the room around us. "I grew up."

Logan didn't. The old Aeryn—Aeryn at the funeral—would have said it.

"I'm happy for you." The new Aeryn has a softer edge.

This is the perfect time for me to walk away. I should encourage her to walk around the club I've carved out of Brooklyn's abandoned subway tunnels. Tell her it's been great seeing her. Wish her a Merry Christmas and get back to my fucking club.

Instead, I ask, "Do you have a minute to catch up?"

Before she can answer, a state senator walks by, tugging the leash of a woman young enough to be his granddaughter. They pause at the nearest conversation pit where she sinks to her knees and starts to suck him off. I'm not sure which is the better actor—her for pretending that his stub of a pencil dick is gagging her or him for groaning like a skyscraper about to collapse.

"Maybe in my office?" I suggest. "It's quieter there."

Her fingers tighten around her glass. "I'm meeting a friend. The man who brought me here this evening."

I don't want to question the hollow feeling that opens beneath my sternum. Fortunately, I keep a professional smile on tap for emergencies. "Of course," I say.

"Here he is now," she says, and I'm not sure if that's relief or regret that spices her words.

The man who steps to her side is half a foot shorter than she is. His dirty blond hair is damp from a recent shower, and his tight black briefs show off an impressive bulge. As he kisses Aeryn's cheek, he eyes a trio of men across the room, paying special attention to the one wearing a necklace of holiday lights shaped like dicks.

"Mr. Lasker," I say, extending a hand like the welcoming host I am.

"Will," he says. "Please."

The last time I saw Lasker at the club, he was spread-eagle on a St. Andrew's cross, putting on a show with a Daddy Dom on the club's main stage in the Heart. I'm willing to bet Kynk's December payroll that his intentions toward Aeryn don't extend to active play.

Nevertheless, Lasker rests light fingers on her elbow as he tells her, "I'm supposed to remind you about your Christmas Eve catering order. Have you decided on dessert?"

Aeryn's lips curve in a smile that's still familiar. "Thanks for looking out for me. I think I'll go with the cranberry tart."

He gives her decision more attention than I think it's worth. His gaze flicks toward me before he asks, "You're sure?"

"Positive," she says. "Thank you for asking."

The guy with the light-up dick necklace laughs, and Lasker's neck whips around like he's caught a left hook. "Then if you don't mind…" he says to Aeryn, his gaze staying glued to the trio across the room.

"Go," Aeryn says, saluting him with her glass.

"We'll meet up at two?"

She snorts. I remember making her produce that sound. She used to cover her face in embarrassment, but Aeryn doesn't look like she gets embarrassed by much anymore. "Please," she says to Lasker. "You'll last longer than that."

He puffs with pride.

"Go," she says again. "I can get home on my own."

This time he *does* manage to peel his gaze away from Dick-light Guy. "Ariel…" he says. There's honest concern in his voice. Honest affection, too.

She laughs. "I'm fine. But thank you. Go play."

Third time's the charm. Lasker brushes another kiss against her cheek before he saunters over to his target.

"How do you know Lasker?" I ask, once he's out of earshot.

"We were engaged to be married," she says. "For about twenty-seven seconds."

"Ouch," I say.

She twitches one shoulder in a shrug before she finally tastes her whiskey. "He was in the closet. And I thought I was up the duff. My brothers would have killed me if Da didn't do the job first—so I figured I might as well come home with a ring on my finger."

I watch her face too closely. "When was this?"

"Ten years ago, come January."

She's watching me too. We both know how to count.

I wish to God she'd taken me up on that escape to my office. Even more than that, I wish I drank while I was on the job.

I step closer to create an illusion of privacy. "Was it mine?"

She eyes me steadily. "It wasn't anyone's. It was stress. I wasn't eating right, wasn't sleeping right. After…"

Logan. So she's not always comfortable saying his name.

She shakes her head, making her hair gleam in the club's flattering light. "It was a long time ago." She squares her shoulders. "So. Do you have time to give me a tour of this place?"

"With pleasure," I say. And I mean it, even more than my tone can convey.

I offer her my arm as we walk the length of the Great Room. My years of owning Kynk have taught me that clients and staff alike will demand my attention if I'm not specifically attending to a guest. Besides, while Aeryn moves in those stilettos like a runway model, a little extra support can't go amiss.

Plus, I want to feel her close by my side.

We make our way past the public playrooms. It's busy tonight, the Friday before a holiday. From the lavish use of toys, it's clear that many people have already opened their Christmas gifts.

Aeryn takes it all in with polite interest. The girl I knew a decade ago would have been shocked by some of what we see.

Not the basic bondage, though. I still remember how hard she came the first time I shoved a gag in her mouth. We had to keep things quiet at the house Logan and I shared in Atlantic City. That gag led to our exploring Aeryn's submissive side— my belt wrapped around her wrists, her first spanking, her learning what good girls get after they drop to their knees on command.

But tonight Aeryn seems surprised by Mistress Cynthia's wax play. And from her wide eyes in the rope room, she hasn't seen a lot of shibari. She's intrigued by the dais in the Heart, by the spanking table and the wide selection of impact toys for very public scenes.

Her glass is empty, so I look for the nearest waiter with a tray of champagne flutes. A quick jut of my chin, and Aeryn is sipping Moët & Chandon, her empty whisky glass spirited away.

She rolls her fingers on the stem of the crystal. I know what a woman looks like when she's aroused, and the lace on that bra leaves *nothing* to my imagination. Ten years ago, I barely had a chance to explore my first love's submissive side. Not the way I could do now. Not the way—

"So," Aeryn asks as I guide her past some of the private playrooms. "Where do you see yourself in ten years?"

I laugh. It's our old game, one we started the first night she slept in my bed. I was desperate to do anything, say anything to keep her from leaving.

Now, I survey the corridor lined with individual dens of depravity. "Right here," I say. "In New York. I love owning the club. I have a company that manages my real estate holdings, so I can handle the hockey team, too."

"The Aces," she says, once again proving she won't shy away from our past.

"What about you?" I ask. "Where are you in ten years?"

"In Chicago," she says immediately. "To keep Da happy. But I'll have my Michelin stars. Maybe a restaurant in New York too. Vegas, if I can find the right property."

"Let me guess," I say. "You'll serve three dozen courses, each with one bite. And everyone who pays a thousand bucks for the pleasure will go home hungry."

"Heathen," she says, elbowing my side.

I resist the urge to catch her arm, to press her up against the distressed brick wall and make her pay for the familiarity.

Before my body overrules my brain, she says, "I've been collecting recipes for years. From Dublin. From every place I could get to in County Cork. I have more than a thousand of them. I want to introduce the world to real Irish food."

"Corned beef and cabbage?"

She frowns. "The flavors, sure. But reworked for fine dining."

She's serious. So I say, "You'll do it then."

I snag another glass of champagne for her, and we head down the hall toward the Parlor. It's a quiet room, a refuge from the rest of the club's chaos. A discreet sign reminds members that this space is intended just for conversation and they're welcome to take other activities elsewhere. Security circulates on a regular basis, inviting people who don't read to move on.

I gesture for Aeryn to take one of the armchairs. My breath hitches when she crosses her legs, leaning back like she's in some corporate boardroom. She raises her glass to me before she drains off half her bubbly wine.

"Where are you in a year?" I ask, because that's the next question in the catechism.

She makes a face. "Opening my first restaurant. For Da's benefit."

I know enough about her father to guess what that means—

a place for Irish mobsters to eat and drink and plot their next illegal move. She'll take in a lot of cash and report even more to the taxing authorities, laundering her clan's dirty money.

"Not much more than a diner," she says, confirming my guess. "Can't be, for Da to be happy. But I plan to keep the kitchen in full view."

"Exhibitionist."

She snorts. "If the shoe fits…" she says, flexing her ankle.

I recognize the invitation. I've been waiting for just that type of opening.

But we're in the Parlor now. And she's finished off the better part of two glasses of champagne, on top of a generous pour of Jameson. And I'd rather she not hate me in the morning. There are very good reasons we haven't spoken in ten years.

So I answer the question she forgot to ask. "In one year…" I say. "The Aces have won the Stanley Cup. Dubois International opens a new hotel on Madison Avenue in the middle of a block I own."

"And Kynk?" her eyes glinting a wicked invitation.

I take the easy way out. "Kynk is getting ready for the Mistletoe Masquerade. Same as every year."

She pouts.

In a desperate attempt to get my mind off those lips, off my memory of exactly what they can do, I ask the last question. "Where are you tomorrow?"

She offers a sardonic smile. "Apparently, I'm alone in my suite at the Waldorf, after a day spent studying some of the finest restaurants in New York City." She eyes me steadily. "But I have until Christmas morning before I have to be back with family in Chicago."

It's still not fair for me to bite. Instead, I ask, "Where are you hosting your Christmas Eve party?"

"Party?"

"The one Lasker mentioned. Where you're serving cranberry tart."

She laughs. "That wasn't a party. That was a get-out-of-jail-free card. We set a code, in case I wanted to leave. If I said *tiramisu*, he promised to get me out of here."

"I'm glad you didn't say *tiramisu*."

"So am I," she says.

I have no business gloating over the fact that she didn't use a safeword. But I do. And I almost miss her next question.

"And you?" she asks. "Where are you tomorrow?"

"I'm having dinner with a dozen billionaires, along with their wives and girlfriends."

"As one does," she teases.

"It's a...club I belong to. The Diamond Ring. We all keep our investments at a tax haven down in Delaware. The owner sets up monthly meetings—part business, part pleasure. Except tomorrow night is all pleasure—a holiday party with plus ones."

"Where do a dozen billionaires go for a holiday party?"

"Rockefeller Center, to see the Rockettes. Then a private dining room at Top of the Rock."

She starts to laugh, but then she says, "Wait. You're serious."

"Absolutely." And then, like I'm a sixteen-year-old kid: "Come with me."

She snaps her fingers. "Just like that? What about the woman you've already invited?"

"There isn't any woman. I was going alone."

"And your tax-haven owner will just accept some plus one he's never met, showing up at the last minute."

"Absolutely."

She wants to believe me. She doesn't.

I take her hand, lacing my fingers with hers. I realize I've been wanting to do that for a long time. "We both know why you're here this weekend. We both miss him. Come to the show tomorrow night. Create one new memory for the Christmas season."

A tremor ripples across her belly. She's close enough that I could slip my fingers beneath the lace band of her panties. I could have that bra off with one quick twist of my wrist.

I can have her tonight. I know that. But I also know I want more.

I meet her gaze—no more words, no more deflection. She's the one who has to decide.

"Yes," she finally says, and I realize I've been holding my breath. "Yes, I'll see you tomorrow."

3

AERYN

W hen I lived in New York and attended classes at the New York Culinary Institute, I spent every spare moment in a restaurant. Morning, noon, and night, I explored new-to-me food. There was always a new flavor to try, another dish to discover.

I never thought about all the other things New York City had to offer. I skipped a visit to the Statue of Liberty. I never went to the top of the Empire State Building. I didn't set foot inside the Metropolitan Museum of Art, or the Guggenheim, or the Whitney. I certainly didn't make time for anything as frivolous as the precision dancing of the Rockettes at Radio City Music Hall.

I was a feckin' eejit.

The Christmas show is glorious. Thirty-six women fill the stage for dance number after dance number. They tell the Christmas story, complete with live animals. They bring full-size tourist buses on stage, dancing on the steps and in the windows.

They dress as identical tin soldiers, turning in military-sharp lines until they collapse in breathtaking slow motion. The last number is one of their famous kicklines, their ankles stretching eyebrow-high as the audience roars with applause.

I join the standing ovation, clapping until my palms sting. "That was incredible!" I say, clutching Gage's arm as the house lights finally come up.

His smile is indulgent. "I'm glad you liked it."

"I loved it!"

He shakes his head. "That's not the way we do things here in New York. You never want to seem *too* enthusiastic."

I try to give him a disapproving glare. "But if I *am* enthusiastic—"

"Let's go, motherf—" Trap Prince starts to say. He's our host for the evening, the billionaire in charge of all the other billionaires. I've known him for little more than two hours, and I've already learned that swearing comes more easily to him than breathing.

But his fiancée, Alix, cuts him off with a sharp elbow to his ribs. "Look at that sweet dress," she says, nodding toward a little girl dressed in Christmas velvet. The child's mother gives Alix an approving nod.

"Let's go, *friends*," Trap corrects himself with a pained smile. "They're expecting us upstairs for dinner in fifteen minutes."

Several people in our party laugh. One man—I think Gage said he's in insurance—fakes a sneeze that sounds suspiciously like the word *whipped.* Alix just clutches Trap's arm and cuddles close to his side. He makes a show of raising his eyebrows in a silent response that stirs something deep beneath my belly. Alix blushes.

Our group follows Trap up the aisle and across the theater lobby. He's a natural leader—broad-shouldered and loud-voiced, with an intensity that makes me understand why a dozen captains of industry have chosen to do business with him.

Not just industry—organized crime, too.

I didn't get a chance to speak with Braiden Kelly—the captain of Philadelphia's Irish mob—before the show began. Gage and I slipped into our seats just as the theater lights dimmed. That was my fault; I kept Gage waiting almost half an hour in the Waldorf lobby as I changed outfits again and again and again.

Da always says I'll be late to my own funeral. I say that's my right, growing up the only girl in a regular gang of heathens. But now it's time to make amends with Kelly, for the benefit of the South Side Squad.

I purposely drop back as our group approaches the elevators in the lobby of 30 Rock. The Philadelphia boss is deep in conversation with a man who is sweating in his winter-weight brown suit. Kelly's gaze is hard as lapis when he finally looks my way.

"General," I say, nodding my head in a gesture of respect. Braiden Kelly isn't just captain of the Philly mob. He's general of all the Irish crime families in America. He's my own da's boss.

The man Kelly was speaking with has taken a step back. I don't know if he's versed in the rankings of Irish mob families. I hope so, because I can't wait to drop my family name. Maybe that will make him break off staring at my chest, as if my Carolina Herrera cashmere turtleneck is some sort of engraved invitation for his drooling attention.

"Aeryn," Kelly says, with a slight dip of his chin. I'm surprised he knows my name. But then I remember it's his business to know everything about every clan in the country. "To what do I owe the pleasure?"

Before I can respond, Kelly reaches past me. "Rider," he says, shaking Gage's hand.

"Of course you two know each other," Gage says. He smiles as he says it, keeping his tone light, but I feel the faint pressure of his fingertips at the small of my back, sending sparks up my spine to the lizard parts of my brain. Gage has followed me across the bronze-and-marble lobby and squared up to Kelly, as if he's willing to fight for my honor if I give him half a sign.

He can't be naive about what such a gesture could cost him. His words prove he knows Kelly's role with the mob. Maybe he just doesn't care. Gage was always good in a fight, for all the years he played hockey. Until that last one. The one that cost Logan his life.

Kelly is eyeing me politely, his eyebrows just raised. I say, "Gage and I are old friends. When he found out I was alone in New York without plans on the Saturday before Christmas, he invited me to tag along."

This isn't a mob function; Kelly holds no actual power at this event. I've fulfilled my duty, recognizing his status with his title. He acknowledges as much by gesturing toward the elevator that has just arrived. "Please," he says to me, letting me enter first. Gage joins us, along with half our party.

The sweat-soaked man squeezes in at the last moment. He stands, facing us, as the elevator soars to the top of the building. I cross my arms over my chest.

Kelly's quick eyes notice, but he merely turns to his wife. "Samantha, this is Aeryn Reardon, from Chicago. Aeryn, Samantha."

Samantha's smile is generous. I've heard stories about her. Every woman born into a mob family has. She serves as Braiden Kelly's Clan Chief—his second in command—a rank no other woman has held.

And yet there's one Irish mob woman with a rank higher than Samantha. That's Fiona Ingram Moran, the ruling Queen of the Boston clan. And she's standing by the hostess stand, talking to Trap Prince like they're old friends. She's part of the Diamond Ring too, a point I would have realized if Gage and I had arrived at the theater on time.

Samantha brushes a kiss against Kelly's cheek. "We'll join you in a moment," she says. "Alix?" She draws the attention of Trap's fiancée, then includes me with a gesture. I smile at Gage before the three of us follow the signs down a short hall to a restroom. Half a dozen gleaming doors sit across from matching sinks. We pause, though, in a softly lit lounge the size of an airplane hangar.

Samantha drops her clutch purse on a ledge in front of a smoked glass mirror. "Alix," she says. "You have *got* to get Roger Turner out of the Diamond Ring."

Alix laughs. "You served as the freeport's General Counsel for how many years? You know Trap will put up with just about anything from his top billionaire clients."

"If that slimy toad delivers one more compliment straight to my breasts, I can't be responsible for what Braiden does."

So, the sweat-soaked man has a name. "Maybe Gage can knock out a couple of his teeth," I volunteer, checking my lipstick in the mirror. "Just as a general service to female-kind," I say.

Alix eyes both of our reflections. "*Frogs* are slimy," she says to Samantha. "Not toads. I'll ask Trap to say something to Turner. Again."

The lounge door opens, and Fiona Moran slips inside. "Are we talking about Roger Turner?"

"Of course," Samantha says.

"Did he bring his wife tonight? I didn't see anyone out there miserable enough to be married to that asshole."

Alix shakes her head. "She sent her regrets last month, when the invitations went out."

"Maybe he isn't really married," Fiona says. She twists her neck as she glances in the mirror, eyeing her arse in her Balenciaga suit. I'd give Gran's recipe for Guinness chocolate cake just to add that outfit to my collection. I realize Fiona isn't wearing anything beneath her tailored jacket. It's a good look, one I need to remember.

"He's married," Alix says. "He's just a horn-dog cocksucker."

Samantha grins at her in the mirror. "I see you're embracing Trap's vocabulary tonight."

Alix shrugs and looks at me. "Sorry, Aeryn," she says. "Once upon a time, I was a respectable girl."

I offer my own shrug. "Sometimes you have to call a gobshite wanker a gobshite wanker." All three of the women laugh.

Samantha runs a finger under her eyeliner as she asks, "So how do you know Gage, Aeryn?"

I choose the simplest answer. "He was my brother's best friend."

Was.

My answer hangs there for a beat too long and I rush to cover the silence. "I hadn't seen him for ages, for almost ten years. But a friend took me to his club last night and—"

"You've been to Kynk!" Samantha's voice is full of sing-song longing, like I've opened a present she hoped to find beneath her own Christmas tree.

Fiona's eyes widen. "What's it really like?" she asks.

"I wasn't... I didn't actually..." A toilet flushes as I fumble my answer. I saw the club, sure. But I didn't really participate. Not after Gage found me at the bar.

Samantha turns to Alix. "*You've* been there. Come on. Spill."

Alix should be laughing. She should be sharing naughty details or—if she's coy—teasing about what she's done in the secret halls of Brooklyn.

Instead, her face has gone still. She stares into the middle of the room, her eyes flat, unseeing.

"Alix?" Samantha asks, her voice suddenly soft with concern.

"Are you talking about Kynk?" comes a voice from across the room. I look up to find a woman wiping her hands on a thick white towel. She's tall like a dancer, and thin like one too. I suspect Roger Turner wouldn't bother staring at her chest; she has the athletic build of a boy. "That's where I met Connor."

"Jaq!" Samantha exclaims, a little too boisterous, a shade too bright. "Tell us what we're missing!" She waves the newcomer over, but part of her attention is still on Alix. As Jaq joins our little circle, Alix shakes off her stillness with a determined shudder.

Fiona pushes for details. "Is there really a stage? Did you play out scenes in public?"

Jaq grins and tosses her towel into a woven basket in the corner. "That first night, Connor took me to his private room."

"And?" Samantha urges.

Jaq wrinkles her nose. "I'm not the type to kiss and tell."

Fiona smiles slyly. "Not even to your new best friends?"

Jaq shakes her head.

Fiona wheedles. "Just tell us what you were wearing."

Jaq laughs. "My old school uniform. Plaid skirt. White top. Knee socks and saddle shoes. All of it about two sizes too small."

Fiona's eyebrows rise. "That sounds like it has potential…"

This time we all laugh—even Alix. But then she fishes her phone out of her pocket. Glancing at the screen, she says, "Text from Trap. He wants to know if we're planning on staying in here all night."

Jaq shoots a shy look at us in the mirror. "Really? That's an option? We can just stay here?"

Samantha squares her shoulders. "If *I* stay, I'll face *consequences.*"

Fiona quips, "You might *consequence* three or four times tonight, if you're lucky."

Jaq looks longingly toward the stalls until Alix touches her shoulder. "You know Connor is lurking in some corner, not saying a word to anyone. We need you to bring out his better side." Her glance takes in all of us. "Let's go, ladies."

The gentlemen stand when we reach our private dining room. Gage pulls out my chair, leaning close to my ear as I settle into place. "I'm afraid to ask what you found to talk about for so long."

"You should be," I say, with a wink. Before he can retort, the servers descend with a first course of Oysters Rockefeller.

The meal unfolds like some sort of fairytale feast. We're a party of twenty-four. There should be glitches in service, food served too cold, wine served too warm. But everything about the meal is perfect—the flavors and the pacing and the relaxed conversation.

Gage listens to my raves about the menu, about the exquisite wine pairings that feature obscure bottles I've never tried before. He never jokes about my hearty appetite, never asks if I have a hollow leg, never questions where I put all the food I'm enjoying.

Jaq and Connor leave first. Fiona's next to go, whispering in the ear of the man she came with, cocking a hip before she bids a sassy Merry Christmas to the room.

Gage clears his throat and swallows the last of his brandy. I pride myself on my ability to take a hint. We say our goodbyes and step into an empty elevator.

"What?" Gage asks, eyeing me in the polished metal door.

"I didn't think I'd have such a good time tonight."

He pretends to take a shot to the heart. "What every man wants to hear."

"You know what I mean," I say, bumping him with my hip. "But honestly, this was perfect. The Rockettes. The meal. The company." The elevator door opens, and we step into the building lobby. "I don't want it to end."

The second the words are out of my mouth, I realize they could make everything awkward. It's nearly midnight. We're both adults. "Not ending" generally leads to one place.

And as attractive as I find Gage Rider, as I've *always* found Gage, I'm not sure heading to his bed is my best option. Not with the anniversary of Logan's death on Monday night. Not when I'm flying back to Chicago on Tuesday morning.

Gage must think the same thing, because he doesn't give me one of his easy golden-retriever smiles. He doesn't wink and act like the consummate host. He doesn't even twist a lock of my hair around his finger, the way he always did ten years ago, when we were working out the choreography for our dance of desire.

Instead, he asks, "You're serious?"

I nod.

"Then I have an idea for one last stop." He pauses as if he can feel the misapprehension that flutters beneath my breastbone. "If, that is, you're up for it."

4

GAGE

Maybe it's the old-fashioned good cheer of the Radio City Christmas show we watched tonight.

Maybe it's the afterglow of some of the most expensive wine I've ever drunk in my life.

Maybe it's the ache of my half-stiff cock, pushing for one more hour, one more glimpse of Aeryn's tight black sweater, of the soft skirt that gets to kiss her thighs, of those totally impractical red-soled shoes.

When she says she's up for anything, I tell Curtis to keep my Rivian SUV waiting at the curb. As we wait to cross the street, I offer my arm to Aeryn. She laughs as a gust of wind catches her heavy wool coat. Right on cue, huge snowflakes begin to fall, like we're starring in some Hallmark Christmas movie.

Hallmark would find a way to get rid of the cartoon characters filling the pedestrian walkway to our destination. There are dozens of them—life size Muppets and Disney princesses and people dressed like Marvel Avengers. They make their money taking photos with gawking tourists, surviving on the tips they glean with their high-pressure pitches.

It's late, and most of the foot traffic is flowing against us. I switch my grip to Aeryn's hand, telling my cock it doesn't mean a goddamn thing when her fingers curl around mine. She's just a girl with common sense, staying close in the crowd.

One more clump of costumed beggars. One more family, three kids crying because of the cold. One more pair of kissing strangers, pushing up against a granite wall, oblivious to the snow that's started to fall in earnest.

"Where—" Aeryn starts to ask, just as we turn a corner. Then: "Oh..."

She's seen it on TV, or in a movie, or in someone's vacation photos on their phone. It's the Rockefeller Center skating rink, complete with Prometheus bringing fire to us cursed humans and an eighty-foot Christmas tree lit up in all the colors of the rainbow.

"Gage..." she says, and I know she sees it the same way I do. It's corny and it's gorgeous and it's the perfect little slice of New York to cap our night. She turns her face up to me. "Can we skate?"

I laugh, because she sounds like she's ten years old.

Her forehead wrinkles, and she punches my arm. "Don't laugh at me."

"I'm not," I lie.

Instead of arguing, she begs. "Please?"

I tell my cock that's not what she's asking for. "Your wish..." I say, making a stupid little half-bow and escorting her down the steps to the warming hut on the edge of the rink. We have to step to the side to avoid a family trudging up to street level, both kids babbling like Santa Claus just gave them a personal tour of the North Pole.

When we get to the hut, a gnome in a scarlet parka is locking a chain across the door. Her raw, chapped hands look like lobster claws in the bright overhead lights.

"Rink's closed," she says, a million wrinkles fanning out around her chapped lips. "Come back tomorrow."

Aeryn whines like someone just sent her to bed without any supper. And my idiot cock thinks *that's* an invitation too.

"Just fifteen minutes," I say to the keeper of the hut.

The crone points to a sign with one scarlet talon. "Nine a.m. to midnight," she says, like I'm too stupid to read.

I reach for my wallet. "You can make an exception."

The witch's lips twist like she's sucking on a lemon. She reaches around the corner of the hut and yanks on some lever I can't see. The rink plummets into darkness.

I take five crisp hundreds out of my wallet. "No one has to know," I say.

She cackles. "You're in the middle of New York City, pal. I let you in, I have to let everyone in."

I add another five bills. "Wait inside the hut," I say. "With the chain across the door. Anyone else who comes to skate will give up and go home."

"And what if my boss shows up? What if he fires me for breaking the rules?"

"If he fires you, I'll give you a new job."

"Doing what?"

"Managing petty cash in my real estate office." I figure if she's fighting a bribe this hard, she'd be great at keeping a lockbox safe from employees looking to boost a couple of bucks.

She twists her neck like a bird eyeing an especially fat worm. Jutting her chin toward the money in my hand, she says, "Add another ten to that, and you have yourself a deal."

I count out the cash from my wallet. I'm short two hundred bucks. "That's it," I say. "I'm tapped out."

She eyes my overcoat. "You got a pair of gloves?"

I dig out a pair of hand-stitched Italian lambskin gloves. They're lined with brown rabbit fur. I hand them over to her, cuffs first.

"Fifteen minutes," she says.

"After we put on our skates."

She looks at both of us, head to toe. "Looks like the two of you forgot to bring your gear."

I point to the sign, the same one that lists the hours. "Rental skates included," I say. "We'll skip the complimentary hot chocolate."

The woman harrumphs, but she slips the chain from its anchors. "Men's on the left," she says. "Women's on the right."

I pass her the eighteen hundred bucks before I usher Aeryn over the threshold.

"Are you crazy?" Aeryn asks as the door creaks closed behind us. Bare light bulbs illuminate the racks of skates.

I grin and shake my head. "I just like getting my way. Go on. Get your skates. I don't trust her not to start the clock before you're out on the ice."

Aeryn looks at me like I've just landed my fourth concussion, but then she shakes her head and moves down the aisle. I stare at her back until she's out of sight.

Standing by the cash register, I think about some of the stories Logan told me about the Reardon family business. Their father, Mickey, likes getting his way too. But he uses a gun to persuade people, instead of a gaping wallet.

Not for the first time, I speculate on my good luck that Mickey Reardon never held me accountable for what happened to Logan. I suspect he never learned the truth about Aeryn and me, or I would have ended up with a bullet at the base of my skull well before I ever got to open Kynk.

Aeryn comes down the aisle, clutching a pair of white leather skates. "Size nine," she says. "Now it's your turn to hurry." She nods toward the men's side of the hut.

I shake my head. "No skates for me."

"But—"

"Let's go," I say, opening the door before she can argue.

The old woman is wiping down the tables, grumbling over a sticky spill of once-hot chocolate. I guide Aeryn to a smooth plastic bench, holding out my hands for her fancy stiletto heels. "You're going to rip those stockings," I say.

"I'd ask you to buy me a replacement pair, if you weren't flat broke."

I chuckle as she shoves her foot into one white boot. She works the laces like a professional skater, automatically pulling them tight for extra ankle support.

"Honestly?" she asks, when both skates are on. "You're not coming out with me?"

The old woman clatters a chair into place at one of the tables. "I think our clock just started ticking," I say, pulling Aeryn to her feet. "Leave your coat." Despite the snow that's falling in earnest, it's a relatively warm night—just a couple of degrees below freezing, if I had to take a guess.

Aeryn eyes me steadily as she unknots her belt. For one idiotic second, I imagine her naked beneath the coat. I picture her peaches-and-cream shoulders, scattered with freckles I once traced in the dark. I wait for the dark flash of her nipples against her high tits.

Her sleek black turtleneck mocks me as she settles her coat on the bench.

"Last chance," she says, holding out one hand.

"Go," I say. "Let's see what you can do."

She can skate. She learned on the same backyard pond Logan did, hitting the ice as soon as she could walk. I've heard all the stories—how her brothers pushed her back and forth as their puck. How she stole Logan's stick one day and refused to give it back until he stood in as goalie. How she challenged her oldest brother to a cross-rink race— and won.

Now she takes a few strokes to find her balance on the rented blades. They probably haven't been sharpened since they were delivered from the factory. For just a moment, I picture arena lights glinting off the sharpest metal in the world. I see a pool of scarlet spreading on the ice, melting it, freezing on it. I start to call Aeryn's name, to beg her to come back, but I bite my tongue just in time.

Her hair streams in the breeze of her speed. Her skirt ripples around her, fluttering against her thighs. She moves faster as she crosses center-ice, gliding farther on each stroke. Her arms rise up in perfect curves and she launches into a flawless double toe loop.

She's stunning out there, an obsidian bird set free. She laughs as she lands a second jump, then she really starts to skate for speed. Even with snow falling, even with the ice chopped up by the night's last skaters, the surface has to be smoother than the pond she learned on. She swoops in an exaggerated oval, keeping her balance on the corners by trailing her fingers beside her gliding skate. Racing to the center of the ice, she spins, her fists pulled into her chest, faster, tighter.

I want to be out there with her. I want to chase her. I want to catch her, to fold my arms around her, to feel her heart beating and her lungs gasping as I tug her close to my chest.

I want to fuck her blind.

I haven't been on the ice since the night Logan died.

Not when I walked away from the Aces. Not when I came back to buy the team. Not for money, not for fun, not for anything I value in this life.

The old woman starts to clang the chains by the warming hut, clattering them against the metal door. Aeryn looks up like a doe caught in a blizzard. Even across the rink, I can see her impulse to ignore the alarm, to keep on skating.

But she tucks her chin toward her chest. She pumps her arms by her sides and skates over to me to clamber off the ice.

Her hair is wild. Her eyes gleam in the shadows. Her smile is bright enough to reach the moon.

"Okay, Rider," she says. "What do we do now?"

5

AERYN

Brushing my teeth on Sunday morning and glaring at myself in a steamed hotel mirror, I try to forget the way Gage stared at me—like he was looking at a ghost.

No. Not a ghost. A zombie. Something from his past that refuses to die, no matter how many times he tries to break free.

Okay, Rider. What do we do now?

It's my own goddamn fault I spent last night alone. I asked a question, when I should have made a statement. I gave a feckin' option, when I should have taken exactly what I wanted.

Gage wanted me. I felt that in his hands when he helped me across the street, and I saw it in his face when my time was up on the ice. I heard it in his voice, when he said, "Now, you get into the car with Curtis, and he'll take you back to the Waldorf. *I'll* take a cab back to Brooklyn."

And stupid me, I went along with his eejit plan—because I'm going back to Chicago on Tuesday morning, because I was afraid of how much I wanted him to touch me, because Logan would have hated everything I've done in the past forty-eight hours.

So, Sunday morning with my hair dried and my makeup perfect, with my Tori Burch skirt and top pulled on like a feckin' uniform, I take out my phone and study my plan for the day. I gave up my reservations at Gotham Tavern for last night's stupid mistake. I call to see if they have a last-minute opening for tonight, and the host laughs so hard he starts to choke.

Fuck him. Fuck all of them.

There's no reason to abandon the plan I built so carefully when I planned this trip from Chicago. Sure, it's Sunday morning, and brunch is a notorious dead-zone for serious chefs. Too many customers want bottomless mimosas with cheap, greasy food to soak up the alcohol. Even the best menus are forced to balance heavy breakfasts with light lunches.

But dim sum is a different thing altogether. Aunt Li is a massive restaurant in Chinatown, taking up three stories of an ancient building on Mott Street. The place is famous for its dumplings, pork sticky rice, and custard tarts. It's as different as possible from the hearty Irish fare I've eaten all my life. I grab the leather-bound notebook I use to take notes and head downstairs for a cab.

Steamed sausage rolls. Shrimp dumplings. Fried turnip cake. I sample all of those, and more. The Chinese family at the round table next to me sees me studying their choices, and they send over the more adventurous dishes: Stewed chicken feet. Steamed beef tripe. Glutinous rice dumplings.

I'm in heaven.

I eat until I can't manage another bite. When the waiter brings my bill, I put down my platinum American Express card, telling him I'm picking up the tab for my new Chinese friends. I leave before they discover my little Christmas present.

That's what it means to be a Reardon, an Irish mob princess. I can take care of the people around me. Da's a millionaire many times over, and he takes pride in providing for his family—all of us, even me, the only girl. I'm thirty-one years old, and I already have a million dollars in my savings account.

Of course that's nothing compared to Gage Rider's billions. If I live to be 80, I'll have fifty-six dollars a day to spend, every day of my life. If I had Gage's money, I'd have twenty-three hundred dollars an *hour*.

So, yeah. The eighteen hundred he gave that woman for me to skate last night was pocket change.

I dig my fingernails into my palms. I don't want to think about skating. I don't want to remember the wind in my hair, the thrill of spinning at center ice almost out of control, the hunger I saw in Gage's eyes when I came back to the bench—I *know* it was there.

Okay, Rider. What do we do now?

I'm a feckin' eejit.

I yank the belt tight on my coat, slip my notebook into my pocket, and head out of Aunt Li's. I don't have another reservation until eight tonight, at Dancing Beet, a vegetarian restaurant on the Upper West Side that's been getting rave reviews.

I could take a cab back to the Waldorf, but I already know I'd just sit in my room and mope. Instead, I decide to walk up Broadway.

I'm wearing Doc Martens, in deference to last night's snow. The laces are tight around my ankles, almost as tight as my skates were last night.

Don't think about skates.

Many of the storefronts I pass are decorated for Christmas. Gold and silver garlands line windows, and colored holiday lights flash around doors. Chinatown gives way to the Bowery, which fades into Greenwich Village.

For a few blocks, I trail behind a quartet of drunken Santa Clauses. Through the window of a coffee shop, I glimpse a grown-up Grinch handing a cup of hot chocolate to a very little Cindy Lou Who. I'm earwormed with Christmas carols—"I

Saw Mommy Kissing Santa Claus" and dogs barking "Jingle Bells" and four feckin' repeats of "Last Christmas".

When my legs get tired, I take a break in a Yemeni coffee shop. They have a fake fireplace against one wall, with stockings hung across the mantel. I think about the silk stockings I rolled down my thighs once I got back to the hotel last night. Just as Gage predicted, the silk was shredded by my skates.

Don't think about stockings.

Fortified by caffeine, I make my way past the Flatiron Building, heading to midtown. I've covered a couple of miles; I'm halfway to Dancing Beet. My toes are cold and my cheeks feel flushed, but for the first time in two days, I'm back in control of my life.

I never should have gone to Kynk with Will. Once I was there, I never should have let Gage order me that Jameson. Once I drank the whiskey, I never should have agreed to a tour of the club. Once I let Gage show me around, I never should have accepted his invitation to meet the Diamond Ring.

There were so many times I could have stepped aside. So many ways I could have taken back my independence. So many chances to remember that I'm Aeryn Reardon, I belong in Chicago, and I have nothing but bad memories from the time I lived in New York City.

But Gage's hands were gentle when he helped me into his massive Rivian. His voice was kind as he told his driver to take me to the Waldorf. His eyes were sad as he softly closed the vehicle's door.

Don't think about Gage.

I'm early for my dinner reservation, but there are seats at the bar. I order whiskey but change my mind before the bartender can grab a glass. I ask for a vodka martini instead, extra dirty. It comes with four olives on a silver pick.

Dancing Beet lives up to its reputation. I order all eight appetizers on the menu, just so I can study the chef's technique. It takes me almost fifteen minutes to identify the flavor folded into my smoked rutabaga carpaccio. It turns out to be minced sea beans.

I take notes. I savor a late-harvest Tokaji instead of dessert. I assure the server I loved the meal, even though I decline to take any of my leftovers back to my hotel.

Back in my suite, I'm forced to stare at the cashmere sweater I wore to Radio City. The skirt, too. They're my favorite winter clothes, and now I want to burn them. They're tainted, ruined by Gage's touch at the small of my back, by his palm on my elbow, by the way he—

Do not think abut Gage Feckin' Rider.

I should be knackered after my long walk. I should be studying my notes for tomorrow's restaurants. I should be packing my clothes, getting a head start on my early-Tuesday-morning departure.

I wonder if Gage is at the club right now. Or maybe he's watching his hockey team. The Aces are on the road, playing in Toronto. He could have taken a private plane up to Canada.

I hate that I know the Aces' schedule. I hate that I still check their standings every morning, exactly the way I did when Logan was still alive. I hate that they're having their best year in a decade, that they're finally in contention for the Stanley Cup.

The press will have a field day if the Aces go all the way this year. Gage will have back-to-back interviews for weeks. Everyone will want to know how it feels to win in this anniversary year of Logan's death.

Do not fucking think about Gage Fucking Rider.

I don't realize I've made a decision until I'm pulling on my sexiest knickers—high-cut black lace, with a trio of tiny red roses centered over each hip. I add the matching bra. I cover up with a Prada knit dress in pine green.

My feet scream when I slip on my Louboutin stilettos. It hurts to be beautiful—that's what Mam always said. I can manage. It's not like I'll be walking the length of Manhattan again.

The doorman hands me into my taxi without a second glance. The cabbie shakes his head in confusion when I give him the address, but he passes me his phone and lets me type in the destination.

As we make our way toward the Brooklyn Bridge, I tell myself I'm being ridiculous. Kynk is a private club. I'm not a member. There is no way in hell I'm getting past the dangerously efficient door dragon, much less the security guards in the lobby.

But I don't tell the driver to turn around.

The shadows framing the door seem darker tonight than they did when I arrived with Will. The walk from the curb seems longer. My fingers hover over the latch for a full minute before I find the courage to step inside.

A stranger sits behind the desk. She's tall and curvy and blonde, and according to the flag pins on her lapel, she speaks different languages than Lydia. But her smile is the identical cool professional greeting as she says, "Good evening."

"I'm Aeryn Reardon," I say.

I'm about to ask her to summon Gage so I can plead my case. But the woman's fingers move before I can beg for help. She taps her tablet, and she nods precisely at what she sees.

"Excellent, Ms. Reardon. I see you're on our guest list. Welcome to the Mistletoe Masquerade."

6

GAGE

"Ho, ho, ho," I bellow from the center of the dais in the Heart, pushing my red Santa cap off my forehead for what feels like the hundredth time. I've skipped the fat suit and the beard for my role in Secret Santa, opting for a tuxedo instead. I'm the only person in the room not wearing a mask.

"I have one last gift in my bag," I announce. "What good little girl or boy is still waiting for a present?"

It isn't Aeryn.

I put her on the list like I was some sort of lovelorn teenager, some pimple-faced loser afraid to ask a girl to Prom. By giving her name to Felicia, I could pretend that I was taking charge of my own fucked-up life.

Too little.

Too late.

Last night, I should have told Curtis to take both of us back to the Waldorf. I should have sent my driver home for the rest of the night, saved myself the long, lonely cab ride back to Brooklyn.

Aeryn *wanted* me to join her. She practically invited me to her room. Keeping some promise to Logan now won't bring him back from the dead.

But I let her go—again. And I didn't pound on her door at three in the morning. I didn't even call her today.

I fucked up.

"Excuse me. Santa? Do you have a gift for me?"

I look down from the dais into the masked eyes of a woman dressed as a black cat. She has streaks of gray in her short, severe bob. Her melon-size tits aren't original equipment; they look absurd with her wasp waist. Her jet-black catsuit accentuates the mismatch.

Aeryn would stop men's hearts in that catsuit.

Mistletoe Masquerade is open to all club members. But Secret Santa requires a little extra holiday spirit—a thousand-dollar donation to my pet charity, Wounded Heroes United. In exchange, submissives get a gift-wrapped box and Doms get their names slipped into one of the Christmas ornaments hung on the tree. Every year, it takes a little backroom recruitment to guarantee an equal number of subs and Doms, but the effort pays off in the end.

Slipping back into my role, I dig into the burlap sack at my feet to produce one final gift. It's wrapped in scarlet paper, with an elaborate green-and-gold bow. I'll have to up my holiday bonuses to the front-desk staff. They did an exceptional job with the gift-wrap this year.

"Let me see, little girl," I joke, making a show out of checking the long scroll Felicia handed me hours ago. "Have you been naughty or nice?"

"Very, very naughty," the sub says, much to the crowd's amusement.

"Then this is the gift for you," I say, after faking another hearty laugh.

Everyone presses closer now. By house rules, no one is allowed to play with their new toys until the last gift has been opened.

The black cat bites her lower lip as she slips a shellacked claw under the ribbon. She puts on a big show of being nervous about stripping away the wrapping paper. Again, when she opens the box.

Aeryn wouldn't fake fear for the crowd.

The cat pales beneath her mask when she reveals a black leather whip.

"Ho, ho, ho!" I say. "Merry Christmas."

The sub looks like she's ready to flee the Heart, to forget all about her prize and escape to the greenroom. But when I gesture toward the Christmas tree, she swallows hard and takes the last ornament.

"Go ahead," I urge. "Open it up, and show everyone your Secret Santa."

Her fingers tremble as she twists the bauble into two half-spheres. A curl of paper nestles in the middle. She catches her breath before she reads out: "M— Master Jonathan."

Aeryn wouldn't stammer.

Jonathan elbows his way to the front of the crowd. He's wearing an elaborate mask with stag antlers dipped in silver glitter. "On your knees, kitten," he commands.

She drops like he shot her. Bowing her head, she offers him the sturdy leather whip. He trails the thong around her neck, and the crowd laughs as she shivers from the tips of her masked cat ears to the curve of her vinyl-covered ass.

I glance toward the wings, ready to signal the servers waiting there with fresh trays of eggnog and vintage champagne. Before I can nod a command, though, a voice cuts through the crowd.

"Santa?"

Aeryn.

I freeze on the dais. Scores of guests catch the drama. In a single breath, the Heart is quiet enough to hear a fucking rein-deer blink.

It's Aeryn. Of course it's Aeryn. I've heard her voice inside my head for ten straight years.

The lingerie she's wearing tonight makes her sexy attire from Friday look like her grandmother's bloomers. Her hair falls in soft waves around her face. She isn't wearing a mask, and her eyes look huge in the Heart's dim light, all pupil with only the faintest rim of green.

She's wrapped a large red bow around her neck.

"Santa?" she says again. "You gave gifts to everyone else. Don't you think it's time to open your own present?"

I own Club Kynk. I'm responsible for the safety and the enjoyment of all my members and their guests. I don't get to play here, not in the public rooms, not in the private spaces, certainly not on the dais here in the Heart.

"Santa doesn't get a present, little girl," I finally say.

"But that's not the way Christmas works. Everyone who's good gets a present."

It's easy to forget we're surrounded by scores of gawking guests. I look straight into her eyes. "I haven't been very good, little girl."

She sinks to her knees in front of the dais. My cock shifts inside my tailored slacks, reminding me of a few items I should add to my Christmas wish list.

"I don't believe that for a minute," Aeryn says.

The energy in the room jacks into the base of my skull like a string of snow-white lights. Everyone knows the rules of Mistletoe Masquerade. Everyone has been waiting to play with their new toys, to explore their new partners. But watching *me*, Kynk's owner, is a hell of a lot more interesting than all the newly opened gifts. Aeryn has them spellbound.

There's no way in hell I can leave her there on her knees, watching, waiting. But before I can figure a way out of this mess, Aeryn says, "Well, even if *you* don't get a present, *I* deserve one."

I play along, jockeying for time. "And what do you want for Christmas, little girl?"

She looks directly in my eyes, like we're alone in the entire world. "You."

7

AERYN

G age takes a step back, folding his arms across his chest. His lips twist into a frown, and he says, "We have rules at Kynk, little girl."

I swallow hard because rejection tastes like bitter melon. But I say, "Of course, Santa."

"Of course, *sir*."

My mouth goes dry as he corrects me. He made me call him *sir* ten years ago. I giggled the first time he ordered me to say it, but it only took one spanking for me to understand the game.

A candle flame flickers beneath my ribs as I repeat, "Of course, *sir*."

"Look around this room, babygirl."

Babygirl. Not *little girl*.

He called me babygirl the first time he made me come. The first time he put me in a gag. The first time he tied me up.

He gazes down at me now. "What do you see, babygirl?"

Glancing over my shoulder, I see women on leashes. Men

stripped down. I see handcuffs and butt plugs and nipple clamps tight enough to make my own chest ache.

But every person looking back at me has one thing in common.

"Everyone's wearing a mask." My knees are starting to burn. I pause for too long, then I remember. "Sir."

"Where's your mask, babygirl?"

"I didn't think to bring one."

He waits.

I'm out of practice. I finally remember to add: "Sir."

"There are masks in the greenroom, babygirl."

"I didn't see them. I was in too much of a hurry to get out here. To offer you a present." My knees throb, and I remember much faster this time. "Sir."

"What do you think should be the penalty for breaking club rules, babygirl?"

I recognize the trick question from the games we played ten years ago. Whatever I answer will be the one thing he'll deny me. So I swallow hard and say, "Whatever you decide, sir."

He nods slowly, his lips barely quirking into an approving smile. He remembers our games too. "A spanking," he says.

The candle flame licks the space between my thighs.

"Five blows," he says.

"Because I skipped a feckin' mask?" My outrage is genuine. I rock back onto my heels. "You aren't wearing one either!"

He waits. I refuse to give him *sir*.

"Ten," he finally says.

"I—"

His eyebrows rise.

We both remember the last time he spanked me, in the living room of the Atlantic City bungalow he shared with Logan. I argued with him then, too, until he ran my total up to twenty. We only got to twelve before our world fell apart.

"Ten," I finally say. "Sir."

"Master Jonathan," Gage says, not taking his eyes from me. "A chair, please?"

A bare-chested giant with a stag's-head mask drags an armchair to the foot of the dais. It takes two men to lift it onto the stage. They shift the Christmas tree back a couple of feet, positioning the chair in the center of a bright, white spotlight.

Gage takes his time settling into the chair. He shrugs his shoulders. Shifts his weight. He spreads his legs wide, and then he snaps his fingers. "Come to Santa, babygirl."

This is wrong. This is filthy. Good girls don't let themselves be spanked. Wise women don't display themselves in public.

But I made my decision the instant I asked the Waldorf doorman to hail me a cab. I merely confirmed it when I offered up my name at the front desk. And I chiseled it in stone when I strode through the club to the Heart.

I strain my thighs, rising to my Louboutin stilettos without touching a hand to the floor. Gage watches me step onto the dais.

He reaches for the red bow I tied around my throat, the one I took from a locker in the greenroom. I shiver when he slides the ribbon across the back of my neck. "Hands," he says, as my nipples turn to stone.

I hold out my wrists, because this is another game we played ten years ago. He lashes my hands tightly, efficiently, binding me palm-to-palm. Before I sprawl across his lap, he pulls his knees together, just a hair.

His thighs are steady beneath me, sturdy. His cock twitches, pressing hard into my belly as I find my balance. If my wrists weren't bound, I'd reach beneath my body. I'd stroke him through his trousers and make him cream his boxers. I'd take whatever punishment he chose to give me after, once he stopped seeing stars.

He smooths my hair back from my face, taking his time to gather it in one hand. Bending over to brush a kiss against my bare nape, he lets his lips linger near my ear. "Say *tiramisu*, and I'll stop."

I manage a nervous grin. "Cranberry tart," I whisper, but I have to swallow hard. "Sir."

He smooths his free palm over my arse, and I feel every stitch of my lace knickers tattooing my heated skin. "Count," he says. "Then *thank you, sir.* Loud enough for them to hear you in the lobby."

I nod, but I'm not sure I'll be able to make myself heard three feet away. I close my eyes.

"Not like that," Gage says. "Eyes open, babygirl. This is why you came tonight. This is what you wanted—everybody watching you."

I can't do it.

He tugs my hair, not enough to hurt, but enough to get my attention. "Don't make this worse than it has to be."

I hear his voice. I understand the words. But I still can't.

"Aeryn," Gage whispers. " Are you choosing *tira*—?"

I open my eyes.

The first blow comes before I expect it. I hear the sound, like a hockey stick breaking, before I register the fire splashed across my arse.

I thought he might go gently, easing me into things, giving me time to remember the past. But he's started at eleven, and every nerve in my body leaps to attention.

Every nerve.

A drumbeat throbs between my thighs. My body remembers Gage's touch. It remembers the excitement of mixing pain with pleasure. It remembers exactly how it feels to hold a safeword, to be the one ultimately in control of exactly how far a scene can go. It remembers power and release and pure, uncomplicated heat.

"One," I say. Then, "Thank you, sir."

"Louder," Gage commands.

He traces the lace across my left hip, circling each red rose with his thumb. I groan as the pressure pulls my knickers tighter against my clit. His second blow is harder than the first.

"Two," I call out. "Thank you, sir."

The pulse between my legs grows faster. My body hasn't forgotten my first time with Gage. My first time with any man.

It was the Friday after Thanksgiving. Logan and a couple of defensemen were taking some homesick Russian rookies out to one of the casinos for caviar and blini after the game.

I drove down with leftovers from a holiday feast I'd shared with fellow culinary students. I had a month off from school. Most of my classmates were working all December, filling in at restaurants during the busy holiday season, but I was late looking for a job and not willing to accept the dregs available once I got my arse in gear.

I let myself into the house on Beach Avenue and put all the food away in the fridge. Settling down to wait for my brother, I started reading a super-hot romance novel on my phone. My hand slipped inside my knickers as the book got spicier. Gage walked in when I was one stroke away from coming.

Now, his fingers tighten on my knickers. He tugs, hard enough to make me gasp. The elastic stings as it snaps back to my arse. Gage's hand lands after that, steady and solid and sharp.

"Three," I cry. "Thank you, sir."

The thrumming in my core spirals up my spine. My nipples are rock hard. My fingers stretch from my bound wrists, quivering with need.

That Friday night ten years ago, Gage saw exactly what I needed. He grinned from across the room and said he could help with that. I told him I was a virgin, and he crossed the room to twist a curl of my hair around his finger. He repeated his offer: "I can help with that too."

I let him.

Here in the Heart, Gage's strong fingers wrap around the triangle of lace that's torturing my arse. The panel between my thighs cinches tight. I cry out from the pressure, and then he twists his wrist, tugging hard enough to shred the delicate lace.

His palm lands low on my arse, close enough to my drenched core that I yelp. My right shoe clatters to the stage. "Four," I call out, desperate for more. "Thank you, sir."

That first time, he didn't gag me. He didn't tie my wrists or use his belt. Those were games we mastered later, in the single month that followed.

Because I didn't go back to New York after that Friday night. Instead, I haunted Atlantic City. Logan and Gage put in long hours at the arena—practice and games and countless hours studying tape. But Gage and I fucked whenever we could, hiding in his bedroom, discovering all the ways I longed to submit, all the ways he knew to own me.

My arse is bare now in the Heart. As he lands his fifth blow, Gage pulls my hair, tilting my chin toward the crowd. He wants me to see them.

I'm on display to every member of the club, subs and Doms, all of them masked, all of them studying the work of a master. All of them measuring out the service of an obedient sub.

"Five," I cry, throwing my voice to the back of the room. My left shoe tumbles to the floor. "Thank you, sir."

We had thirty days before we were caught. Thirty days before our lives spun out of control. Thirty days before I told him I hated him, before I said giving him my v-card was the biggest mistake of my life, before I screamed I never wanted to see him again.

I lied. I wanted him even then. I've dreamed about him ever since. I've never been with another man who could read the tiniest hints of my body, who could measure out precisely how much I can bear. No other man has ever known me better than I knew myself. No one has been as good as Gage.

"You're so red," he growls, just before his palm lands on the right cheek of my arse.

"Six," I call, obedient even though my throat feels torn. "Thank you, sir."

He's hard beneath me. I'd forgotten the length of his cock, the girth. I want to beg him for it, make him promise he'll feed it to me, then he'll fill my aching pussy once my punishment is done.

But good subs don't ask for what they want. Good subs trust their Doms. Good subs get rewarded when they follow the rules.

My left cheek ignites from the flat of his hand.

"Seven," I croak, the loudest sound I can make. "Thank you, sir."

I can smell myself, slick with need. He told me once I smelled like salt air. I tasted like honey, he said, but smelled like the sea.

His hands are scarred where he caught too many pucks. A thin white line slices through his eyebrow, reminder of some long-ago game.

He smacks the same place he did after ripping off my knickers, the bruised hot flesh so close to my core.

"Eight," I moan, stretching my arms like they can reach an invisible light switch. "Thank you, sir."

The same place, again. Every muscle in my body is taut. My fingers spasm. My toes point. My thighs feel like they're roasting over an open flame.

"Nine," I whisper. "Thank you, sir."

"Look at all the people, babygirl," he growls. "They're here to see you grovel. They're here to see you beg. Tell them what you want from me. Tell them what you need."

They're watching. People with cat masks, with sequins, with horns and with wires. Everyone came for the Mistletoe Masquerade, but they've stayed to watch me.

They can hear my ragged breath. They can smell me—salt and honey and sweat. They can see me, legs stretched, grinding my mound into the hard, iron heat of Gage's covered cock.

"Whatever you desire." I shape the words with my lips,

barely able to speak them out loud. "Sir," I add, drawing out the syllable on a sigh.

"Good girl," he says. And his palm lands, harder than I dreamed I could take, sweeter than any punishment I ever imagined for myself.

Gage knows me. He's weighed my strength to the ounce, to the gram. The spiral cord inside me unravels. My heartbeat thunders down my spine to pool between my legs, filling me, overflowing. Every stretched muscle in my body releases at once, and I pull apart at the seams.

"Ten," I sob as my world spins apart. "Thank you, sir," I gasp as my soul shatters.

8

GAGE

"Hush," I say, gathering Aeryn close to my body. With my arms folded around her, I unwrap the red ribbon from her wrists. "I've got you, beautiful. You're fine, sweetheart. You're safe."

She's sobbing like a child, clutching at my tuxedo jacket, burying her face against my snow-white shirt. I touch my lips to the crown of her head, then smooth her hair down her back, all the while murmuring words of comfort. I'd forgotten how she looks when she falls apart. How she loses all her sharp edges, all her steel.

"Hush," I say again, pulling her even closer.

The Heart is coming back to life. Anyone who's spent any time at Kynk knows the importance of respecting a scene, of not interrupting a Dom and his sub. Concentration is vital—a distracted Dom could overstep his sub's boundaries without any intention to do harm.

But club members are free to move now. Some retreat to the

public playrooms where they can try out their Secret Santa gifts. Others head back to the Great Room for a drink and a leer. A few conversations launch with whispers, and someone laughs in the corridor outside the private rooms.

Aeryn buries her face against my chest. "I'm sorry," she whispers. I feel her words more than hear them.

"I'm not." I tighten my arms around her.

"I— I never cry like this. I... I've never done that before. In front of people, I mean. It was so...intense."

"You were magnificent."

She shifts on my lap, her bare ass riding the hard-on I haven't managed to deflate. "Oh, Gage," she sighs, and *that's* my Christmas present, hearing my name on her lips.

She reaches between us, but I catch her wrist before she can stroke my cock.

"Let me," she says.

I shake my head. "I'm fine."

"I *want* to—"

I lower her hand to her side with enough force to remind her that I'm the one in charge. "I have a reputation to maintain."

A wicked glint flashes in her eyes. "Trust me. Your reputation will only be enhanced when they see that thing."

I curl my finger under her chin. Her smile is a work of art. "Let *me* take care of *you*," I say.

She huffs a little protest, but she drops her attempt to service me. My cock twitches its rebellion. It wouldn't take much to get relief—those fingers, that mouth, that sweet, sweet pussy...

But I wasn't lying when I mentioned my rep. I need my customers to respect my authority, to understand that my rules always matter. I'm not one of the crowd. If they ever see me hip-deep in a sub, they won't think of me the same way again.

"Can you stand?" I ask Aeryn. Obediently, she tries, swaying on legs that have been pushed to their limit. I cup my hands under her elbows, relishing her weight as she steadies herself with fingertips to my shoulders. "Good girl," I say.

Her blush is like sunrise.

I have a club to manage. A Masquerade to maintain. But the clock is ticking closer to midnight and members will be leaving soon, calling it a night, heading home for more mundane holiday festivities. It's Sunday, and tomorrow is Christmas Eve.

I wrestle a cell phone out of my pocket. "Flynn," I say when my chief of security picks up on the first ring. "I'm heading out early. Call if any emergencies come up."

"There won't be any emergencies, boss."

There won't be. That's why I pay Flynn like a C-suite executive of a Fortune 500 company.

Aeryn is steadier on her feet now, but she's starting to shiver. I shrug out of my jacket and drape it over her shoulders. She pulls the lapels close, setting her teeth to keep from chattering.

I collect her shoes and the damp black scrap that used to be her panties. She holds out her hands for her things, but I shake my head. The panties go in my pocket, next to my cell phone and keys. I dangle her shoes from two fingers as I lead her out of the Heart.

As I expected, the Secret Santa participants are putting their holiday gifts to good use. A few of the couples in the public playrooms have garnered spectators, but the crowd is thinning rapidly. My bartender stands alone in the center of the Great Room. Over in one of the conversation pits, two men are pumping some ropy Christmas cheer over a woman wearing nothing but a mistletoe collar. The rest of the space is empty.

When we reach the greenroom door, I brush Aeryn's hair from her face. "Are you okay to get dressed on your own? I can send someone in to help."

"I'm fine," she says. As if to prove her words, she leans in for a kiss. Her lips part before mine do. I may own the club, but I'm not made of fucking steel. I cup the back of her neck and draw out the kiss until she moans into my mouth.

"Go," I say, pulling back enough to catch a lock of her hair around my finger. She tries to steal another kiss, but I force myself to step away. "Take your time. I'll meet you in the lobby." I hand over her shoes like a man giving away a fortune.

She passes through the door to the greenroom, my tuxedo jacket swaying over the curve of her ass. The black wool covers my handiwork, but I know her creamy skin must be flushed crimson. She'll be bruised by morning, something I'd apologize for if I didn't know how much she'll crave the reminder of what she endured.

Aeryn was always brave—letting me be her first, allowing me to gag her, then pushing for so much more.

But she has a quality that makes her even more valuable as a sub: She *trusts*. Once she's committed to a Dom—to me—she shimmers with absolute faith in his commands. I don't know another woman who could do what she did tonight—find the nerve to come to the club in the first place after ten long years, then take the full force of an unrestrained spanking in front of strangers.

She did it for me. Because I knew she could.

The door closes, and I curl my fingers into fists to keep from following her into the greenroom. *That* would give Kynk an unexpected holiday spectacular—Flynn wrestling me out of my own club's safe space. He wouldn't hold back as he dragged me down to the cell in my own office. Rules are fucking rules.

Aeryn will need a few minutes. That gives me time to swing by said office, to pick up a few necessities and log out of my computer.

Back in the lobby, I text Curtis and tell him to bring around the car. After that, I chat with Felicia, asking about her holiday plans. Kynk is closed two days a year—Christmas Eve and Christmas Day. I didn't set the calendar because of anyone's religious beliefs. I've just learned over the last eight years that Christmas has a way of locking down even the strongest kinks.

Aeryn finally steps out of the greenroom looking exactly like what she is—a submissive who just experienced the most earth-shaking orgasm of her life. Her lips are swollen from our kissing. Her hair is tousled. Her eyes look sleepy, even though she smiles when she sees me.

She's wearing a dark green sweater dress, covered by her wool coat. My jacket is folded over her arm. Her ankles sway in her stilettos.

I brush my fingers against the torn lace in my pocket. She shivers, as if we're connected by a live electric wire.

"Have a good night, Felicia," I say, not taking my eyes off Aeryn.

"Good evening Mr. Rider. Ms. Reardon."

Both security guards step forward to open the door.

Curtis waits at the curb. Aeryn climbs into the back first, sucking in a sharp breath as she settles on the leather seat. I bite back a gloating grin. *I* did that. *I* set her flesh on fire. All because she trusts me.

As Curtis takes his place behind the wheel, he finds my gaze in the rear-view mirror. He's waiting for instructions, for a destination. I'm waiting too.

Aeryn doesn't hesitate. She leans into my side and whispers, "Let's go home."

I let out a caged breath, surprised to discover how much I care. "Home," I say to Curtis, and I press the button that raises the privacy screen

Aeryn needs food and drink, and she needs salve on her bruising skin. She whines, though, when I lean forward to open the cooler across from our seat. There's champagne in there and a bottle of Grey Goose, a bottle of Glenfiddich too. But I skip over those and crack open a bottle of Voss water, helping her hold it so she can drink.

If we were already home, I'd give her raspberries and Brazil nuts, or I'd break into my stash of free trade dark chocolate. But she needs something now, so I take out one of the protein bars I grabbed from my office. I break it into three pieces before I peel open the wrapping. She opens her mouth like a baby bird and lets me put food on her tongue.

I grabbed a tin of arnica cream, too. The scent of sage and rosemary throws me back ten years—it's the same stuff the Aces' trainers used on us after every hockey game. It's the brand I bought a decade ago, the week after Thanksgiving, when I first tied Aeryn to my bed.

I could wait until we reach my condo, but I don't want to. Aeryn's still shivering, despite her coat and her wool dress, despite the water she's drunk and the food she's eaten. She's deep into sub drop now, and I need another way to remind her body that she's safe.

It's awkward, pulling her onto my lap in the back of the Rivian, and I'm certain she's flashing back to the Heart. But I keep my hands gentle as I shift her garments, barely touching her hot, red skin as I discover the extent of her need.

The arnica is cool on my fingertips as I scoop it from the tin. Aeryn's whimper turns to a sigh as I smooth the cream over her ass, a thin coat at first, giving the herb a chance to sink in.

I've scarcely straightened her clothes when the car approaches the gate to its underground garage. I know the routine like I know how to brush my teeth—the pause on the ramp as Curtis lowers his window to enter a code, the smooth move forward after the metal door rises. Without my asking, Curtis stops in front of the private elevator that takes me to my penthouse. He opens the car door on Aeryn's side and offers a hand to help her out.

"Thank you, Curtis," I say. "We'll stay in for the rest of the night. In fact, go ahead and take off tomorrow. We don't have plans for Christmas Eve."

"Yes, sir!" he says, his face brightening past his usual professional discipline. "Merry Christmas, sir!" He ducks his head toward Aeryn, who still clutches her bottle of water. "Ma'am," he says, touching an imaginary cap.

I have her in the elevator before Curtis has parked the

Rivian in its designated slot, and I punch in the code that takes us to the thirty-third floor. Another six digits let us move from the private elevator landing into the condo's formal foyer.

A wall of windows looks out over the Brooklyn Bridge. The Empire State Building glows in the distance, its spire lit in red and green for the holiday.

"Oh my God," Aeryn breathes.

"A little different from Beach Avenue, isn't it?" I take her coat and hang it in the closet. She gapes at the maple cabinetry, at the snow-white couches and the sculpted chairs arranged in clusters of three and four. She's drawn to the panoramic windows like a steel needle to a magnet.

"This is amazing," she says. Her gesture takes in everything —the wall of hardback first editions and the stereo system worth my entire rookie-year salary, the shimmering wet bar with more bottles than most restaurants.

"I'll give you the full tour in the morning," I say.

She starts to demand one now, but her jaw cracks into a yawn. She laughs and says, "I'll hold you to that."

I take her hand as I walk her down the hall. We pass four guest rooms, each with a king-size bed and an ensuite bath, each decked out with thousand-count cotton sheets and towels the size of a hockey net.

She'd be comfortable in any one of them. Safe. Secure. But I don't want her hidden behind a closed door. I want her next to me. Under me, if I thought she was in any shape to take it.

"Get rid of those things," I say, nodding toward her shoes as we reach the master bedroom. I switch on the lamp on the nightstand. She sighs as she steps out of those red-soled torture devices, then offers a grateful little mew. I almost miss her exhausted smile because I'm digging in the chest of drawers.

Tossing things on the bed, I turn back to catch her swaying on her feet. "Easy there," I say, steadying her with a palm to her elbow.

I gather her hem in my hands, skimming the soft green wool

over her body. Without my asking, she raises her arms, slipping free from the dress, which I drape over a chair by the window. She reaches behind to unclasp her bra, but I get there first. I ease the straps down her shoulders, peeling away the lace to drop it on top of her dress.

Her tits are as perfect as ever and another night, I'd already have one in my mouth to see if I can still make her come with just the scrape of my teeth. But gooseflesh is rising on her arms, and she's chewing on her lower lip like she owes me some decision.

Turning to the bed, I retrieve the Aces T-shirt I tossed there. It's tight on me, which means she ends up wearing it like an artist's smock, the hem hanging halfway down her thighs. I tell myself not to stare at the stylized playing card splayed across her chest, at my team's name written in teal-and-purple script.

She stands still while I toe off my shoes and socks. My trousers fall over the chair next to the one holding her dress. My bowtie, too. I scrabble at cufflinks and studs before I yank the shirt over my head and drop it on the pile.

Modeling my black silk boxers, I consider getting her a pair as well. But she's in no condition to balance on one foot, then the other, pulling them on. And despite my very best intentions, I don't trust myself to kneel in front of her and pull them up myself.

Besides, her well-spanked ass doesn't need another layer of cloth.

I walk her over to the bed and pull back the covers. She climbs up with the simple faith of a child. I settle her on her side, head on one down pillow, another hugged to her side like a teddy bear.

Turning off her lamp, I walk around the bed in the dark. I hear her catch her breath as I climb in beside her, and she holds it while I turn to my side. I'm the big spoon, taking care not to press too close to her ass, but I gather her hair off her neck and work my fingers along the tight muscles of her nape.

She sighs and relaxes against me, her spine curving toward my chest.

We should talk. We have ten years of missing conversations to catch up on, a decade of pain to boil off. We need to go over this evening—why I left her name at the front desk, why she chose to come to the club, all the things I made her do, and all the reasons she did them.

Impossibly, I'm still her Dom. I need to keep our lines of communication open. I need to keep her safe.

But that's the very reason she needs to sleep tonight. We can talk tomorrow.

So I brush my lips against her shoulder. I whisper, "Thank you. For everything."

I wait for her to whisper something back. But she's already settled into the steady, deep breaths of sleep.

9

AERYN

I wake to sunshine streaming through floor-to-ceiling windows. Gage's side of the bed is cold, and the bedroom door is closed. I wonder how long he's been awake.

Even more, I wonder how much I'd pay for a toothbrush, a steaming hot shower, and a pair of thick, fleece sweatpants.

I laugh when I stumble into the bathroom, because Gage has read my mind. A toothbrush sits beside the sink, still wrapped in its cardboard-backed plastic. It takes me more than a minute to pry the thing free, but it's worth the effort.

A shower's next, and Gage's doesn't disappoint. I shouldn't be surprised by the plumbing a billionaire can demand, but the six adjustable nozzles leave me impressed. There's a creamy bar of milk-white soap, and I lather up three times. He only has one of those feckin' shampoo-and-conditioner blends that men seem to love, but I cut him a bit of slack. My hair comes away clean and sleek.

Back in the bedroom, I don't even consider putting on my

dress. Instead, I head into a closet that's the size of some small European countries. It takes me a few minutes to sort through drawers, but I come away with a pair of sweatpants in Aces teal that I can cinch tight at the waist. Another field trip yields a purple sweatshirt that fits me like a tunic. I roll up the sleeves four turns and do the same with the pants. I have to raid the dresser to find a pair of thick, white socks.

Throughout it all, I'm aware of a dozen aches and pains in my body. My arms feel like I've done a thousand push-ups. My sides complain when I twist to either side and my thighs are tired, as if I've run every step in Wrigley Field.

But my arse feels fine. A little sore, if I push on it with my fingers, a little warm to the touch, but fine. That arnica cream always did work miracles…

Running my fingers through my damp hair, I make my way down the hall toward the front of this luxury home. Before I can step into the living room, though, I hear Gage's voice, sharp with frustration.

"Jesus, Trap. Stop laughing. Trap! Christ!"

He must be talking to Trap Prince, the man who treated us to the Rockettes show and dinner on Thursday night.

Gage lowers his voice. "I'm just saying, I know you have a place here in the city." He sounds like he's explaining simple addition to a child. "And I know you bring Alix to that place. And I suspect you've bought her a present or two while you're up here. So if you can point me toward wherever you've gone to find one of those goddamn presents—"

Trap must take mercy on him, because Gage chokes off his explanation.

"Gallagher Samson," he says after a moment, with a tone that says he's repeating information from Trap. "Fifth Avenue. Do you know how late they're open today?"

Even from my perch in the hallway, I can hear Trap's explosion. He isn't a cocksucking secretary. And he doesn't have a motherfucking clue if Gallagher Samson is open. And if Gage wasn't such a cheap-ass jizzstain, he would have done his shopping earlier than the day before Christmas.

"Thanks, Trap," Gage says when the tirade runs down. "I appreciate the help. Yeah. Merry Christmas to you too. Give my best to Alix."

He's putting away his phone when I venture around the corner.

"Hey," I say. This is the moment I'm supposed to feel shy. After all, I tied a feckin' red bow around my neck and offered my body to this man. I let him tie me up and spank me raw. I called him Sir as he made me come in a spotlight in the center of a stage, surrounded by strangers.

But he's *Gage*. The first man who ever fucked me. The first man I ever loved.

The man I have a sneaking suspicion I might love still, because of everything that's kept us apart for the last ten years, because of everything that ever brought us together.

"Hey," he says.

I cross the room and kiss him. He tastes like peppermint and coffee. His hair stands up in short, sharp tufts, and I laugh when I finally step away. "I *really* must have been out of it. I didn't hear you shower."

"I used one of the guest baths," he says. "I wanted to let you sleep."

"I needed it," I say.

"You deserved it." And *that's* what makes me blush, those three words in that rough tone—acknowledging everything we did together without apology or shame. He follows up with a grin. "Hungry?"

"I'm starving."

"Have a seat,' he says, gesturing toward the dining room table, which is larger than the kitchen counters in some restaurants I've worked in. "Start with some orange juice. I'll be out in a minute." And he disappears into the honed-maple kitchen.

Something smells amazing. There's coffee and the mouthwatering scent of hot bread baked with chocolate and the smell of melted butter and something that has to be mushrooms—chanterelles, I'm pretty sure. I've spent the past week eating three meals a day in the finest restaurants available in New York City, but my stomach feels like it's been empty for years.

I sip at my orange juice and call into the kitchen, "Can I help?"

"Nope." Gage appears with a thermal carafe and a napkin-covered basket. He sets down the latter and pours me a cup of coffee before heading back into the kitchen.

Of course, I peek. The basket is filled with pain au chocolat, each flaky rectangle oozing twin pools of rich, dark filling.

Gage comes back with two plates. He puts one in front of me—an egg-white omelet, stuffed to perfection with frilly crisp-edged mushrooms. As I lean forward to take a deep sniff, I catch a whiff of nutty gruyere cheese.

"Nobody ever cooks for *me*," I say.

"I expected as much."

"Where did you learn to do this?"

"The omelets? I've been loading up on protein since before the Aces called me up."

I remember him blending viscous shakes in the Beach Avenue kitchen. He and Logan pounded down three of those things a day. "And the bread?" I say, helping myself to one of the treats in the basket.

He grins. "You can get anything delivered in New York City. I thought I remembered you like a good pain au chocolat."

"You remember everything," I say, licking a dollop of chocolate off my thumb.

He stares at my mouth as I swallow. "I do."

Something flips strong and hard inside me.

"Eat up," he says. "We have places to go. People to see."

I make short work of my breakfast but Gage still eats like he's being chased by a freight train. I wonder if he actually chews his food before he swallows.

"Let's go," he says, when I lift the final flake of pastry off my plate with my index finger.

I stand beside the table. "You cooked. I'll do the dishes."

"The dishes can wait."

"Let me at least run water over them."

"I'll do that," he says, frowning at my feet. "Go look in my closet. There's a pair of flip-flops in there somewhere."

I look out the window at the glistening city. "It's December in New York City. I'm not going anywhere in flip-flops."

"You won't be wearing them very long."

There's another one of those flips, despite the ballast of an excellent breakfast. I very much want to know what Gage is planning.

He refuses to say anything, though, just sends me back to his closet. There *is* a pair of flip-flops, buried in the back, but I'm pretty sure I'll break my neck if I try to wear them.

Instead, I change back into my dress. I have my bra, but I'll have to go commando. At least my Louboutins feels familiar on my bare feet.

Gage frowns when I return to the living room. "I preferred your other outfit."

I shrug. "You take what you can get."

"I do. Don't I?"

He sounds so pleased with himself that I flash him a middle finger. For a moment, I think he'll make me pay for my brattiness. Instead, he glances at his watch and says, "Let's go."

In the foyer, he holds my coat for me, and then he leads the way to the private elevator. I start to head toward the Rivian across the garage, but Gage redirects me toward a deep red Porsche, his palm at the small of my back.

Driving a sports car in New York makes even less sense than driving one in Chicago. Gage, though, has the enthusiasm of a teenager behind the wheel. He works his way over the bridge into Manhattan like he's playing some sort of video game. I pretend I didn't overhear his conversation with Trap as we wind our way toward—presumably—Fifth Avenue.

The further we move uptown, the more elaborate the Christmas decorations. Some stores' displays are stark and dramatic. Others light up with elaborate dioramas from Christmases past.

Gage finally pulls into a space labeled as a loading zone. The shop's four windows are hung with simple white lights. Each one features an ornament-laden tree—crimson balls on one, blue angels on another, gold stars on a third, and silver snowflakes on the last. They're simple. Elegant. Classy.

"You can't park here," I say.

"They'll only ticket. Not tow."

"Gage…"

"Aeryn."

I give up and walk into Gallagher Samson.

The boutique lives up to the promise of those holiday windows. Clothes are displayed on simple racks, with plenty of space to browse the merchandise. A woman hurries over from the register to greet us.

She's dressed like my eighth-grade English teacher at St. Boniface, in a boxy lavender suit. Her pink silk top features an elaborate bow at her throat. She wears support hose and practical shoes, and her shock of white hair is twisted into a bun. A brooch shaped like a reindeer weighs down her lapel, gold with a single small ruby for its nose.

"May I help you?" she asks, her voice as warm as cinnamon tea.

"I phoned this morning," Gage says. "I'm Gage Rider. I'm a friend of Trap Prince."

"Of course, Mr. Rider," the woman says, her pale blue eyes glinting as if he's just told her a joke. "I'm Martha Gallagher."

"Ms. Gallagher," he says, like a line chef hoping to impress with his first rendition of hollandaise.

"Martha," she corrects him with a laugh that sounds like

holiday bells. "Please. And you must be Ms. Reardon." She turns to me.

"Aeryn," I say, reaching out to shake her hand.

"Aeryn," she repeats, then claps as if my name delights her. "I've taken the liberty of pulling a few things you might find of interest."

I glance at Gage with a look of disbelief. I've been with him since he got off the phone with Trap Prince. Even if he sneaked in a phone call while he was making me breakfast, this joyful little woman has had less than an hour to prepare for our arrival.

Gage offers an elaborate shrug, both hands turned toward the ceiling.

"Right this way," Martha says, ushering us toward the back of the shop.

"I'll wait up here," Gage says.

"You're welcome to have a seat outside the fitting room. I just mixed up a fresh batch of eggnog."

"I'll wait here," Gage repeats, his voice a little rough.

He's embarrassed. This man—who runs a sex club catering to every kink under the sun, who turned me over his knee without blinking, who served me breakfast this morning like not a day has passed since we fucked like bunnies for the hottest month of my life—he's blushing at the thought of watching me try on clothes.

In a rush, I realize it's not my body that makes him uneasy. It's the thought of buying me a present. That's an intimacy we've never shared before.

"Well," Martha says. "Just let me know if you need anything." And she whisks me back to the fitting room as if she's taking me to a royal ball.

She's done her work well. A display rack stands beside a triple mirror, filled with party dresses. There's hand-embroidered emerald silk and ruched cobalt satin and black chantilly lace over a floor-length ruby shell. There are metallic florals and pearly scallops and a leather dress that looks too short for an elf. Martha flips through them all, rearranging the hangers, sorting them by some secret system. Three times, she transfers a dress to another rack, saying, "No," and, "Not right at all," and "It was a long-shot anyway."

In the end, she hands me a floor-length dress cut from lapis-color crepe. It's sleeveless, with a single silver button at the asymmetric neckline. The dress gathers in gentle folds across the waist, drawing the eye away from a hidden zipper.

"Try this one, dear," Martha says.

I step into the fitting room, leaving the door ajar. "I appreciate all the work you've done on such short notice," I say as I shrug out of my coat.

"I love pulling together collections like this," she says.

"You certainly have some beautiful things to choose from." I step out of my shoes and tug off my dress.

"Why thank you, dear," Martha says with a laugh. And then, "Oh my…"

For one uneasy second, I think she's seen my bruises from last night. But then she clicks her tongue three quick times and shakes her head with a fluttery little laugh. "I'm sorry, dear. You'll need something under that dress."

My cheeks turn scarlet. It's a sign of her hospitality that I forgot I have no knickers. "I'm sorry—" I start to apologize, but she only waves a wrinkled hand.

"None of that," she says with a bright smile. "You wouldn't believe how often my customers lack appropriate underthings." She trills another laugh and slips out of the fitting room. She's gone for less than a minute before she returns with a pair of simple cotton briefs.

She busies herself with the sapphire gown as I pull on my new knickers. "Now," she says, passing me the delicate dress. "Let's see how this looks."

It looks amazing.

It looks like every stitch was made specifically for my body.

The waistline traces my curves like a lover. The color turns my hair into shining bronze. My eyes deepen to a green not found in nature. My shoulders—naturally broad—look delicate but strong.

"It's gorgeous," I breathe. I don't know where I'll wear it, but it has to be mine.

"It *is* stunning," Martha says. "But maybe we'll like the next one even more."

"No," I say, shaking my head as I look over my shoulder into the mirror. "I won't like anything more. This is perfect."

Martha brings me shoes—sedate sandals that are infinitely more comfortable than my stilettos. She offers a simple pearl choker as well, along with matching earrings. I half-expect her to summon a crystal coach, like an honest-to-God fairy godmother.

"There," she says before offering a sly wink. "Shall we keep all of this a surprise for Mr. Rider?"

"Yes, please," I say.

And that's what we do. I find Gage at the front of the store, where he's watching a uniformed meter maid slip a parking ticket under the Porsche's windshield wiper. "I told you!" I said.

"Cost of doing business," he says. "Did you find something?"

I suddenly feel shy. "Yes."

"Good."

Martha calls him over to the register, and he works some magic with a black American Express card. "Thank you," I say to Martha as Gage collects a bag brimming with silver tissue paper.

"My pleasure," she says. "I can't think of a better way to spend Christmas Eve." Her joyous laugh follows us out of the store.

Gage opens the Porsche's passenger door, but I feel awkward folding into the sports car. My coat almost catches in the door, and my shoulder twinges when I twist around for the seatbelt.

I can't think of a better way to spend Christmas Eve.

I can. I've spent Christmas Eve the exact same way the last ten years—getting drunk on whiskey, toasting Logan's memory. I owe that to my brother, to never forget my role in how he died.

Shaking my head, I remind myself that none of this can last. This trip to New York is a farewell to my old life. I head home to Chicago tomorrow, to open the diner my father demands, to take my place as a loyal Reardon daughter.

Christmas Eve.

I've let myself be seduced by skyscrapers and fine dining, by a stunning crepe gown and the force of nature that is Gage Rider. I shouldn't have any of this. This is the very opposite of what I deserve.

Of all people, Gage should understand we've made a mistake. He has the same memories I do. He survived the same Christmas Eve that destroyed me.

Gage smiles at me through the windshield before he deposits the Gallagher Samson bag in the car's compact front trunk. He plucks the parking ticket from the window and slips it into his back pocket. Sliding into the driver's seat, he turns to me with a reckless grin.

"Where to, next? I was thinking Tiffany's."

"I don't need any more presents."

"I know you don't *need* them. But I want to give them to you."

I wring my hands. "I don't have anything for you."

"You already gave me a gift, wrapped it in a big red bow. And I fully expect a private runway show of whatever is in that bag."

I stare out the window.

"Aeryn?" Gage finally says.

I twitch a shoulder to let him know I heard.

"Did I say something wrong?"

I shake my head.

"Did I make a mistake?"

Another shake. Even without turning around, I know he's studying me. I can picture his narrowed eyes. I pull myself closer to my door, in case he thinks he can just reach out and make it all better.

"Babygirl," he says, sticking to his side of the car. "I can't read minds."

"It's Christmas Eve," I finally say. And when he doesn't respond, I continue. "I mean, I know how to read a feckin' calendar. I knew the date when I woke this morning. For God's sake, I'm heading back to Chicago tomorrow, to spend Christmas with the Reardon clan, the way I have every year of my life. But hearing Martha say it… It was ten years ago, Gage. Ten years ago *tonight*. Dresses and Tiffany's and prancing around in everything you just bought me… It's not right. It's not fair. We can't forget losing Logan."

"I haven't forgotten a thing," he says, his voice dangerously soft.

"But…" I wave my hand toward the trunk and my beautiful new clothes.

"What do you want to do, Aeryn? What can you possibly think will make it all right?"

I say the words before I have time to regret them. "I want to go to Aces Arena. I want to see where Logan died."

10

GAGE

With holiday traffic, it takes almost four hours to drive to Atlantic City.

Four hours of absolute silence.

Four hours to think about everything I've done over the past four days, since Aeryn Reardon walked into my club. Four hours to think about everything I've done over the past ten years.

I used to wake up from screaming nightmares about Logan bleeding out in front of that goal. I had to skate the length of the ice, but my blades melted away beneath me. I had to scrape up all his blood, and he'd die if I missed a drop. I had to make him say my name; if he said it I could bring him back from the dead, but he just punched me, breaking me open like a blood-filled balloon.

The nightmares finally stopped when I bought the team—but that didn't mean I forgot him. There hasn't been one single day that I've walked into Aces Arena and not remembered Logan Reardon. I see him suiting up for practice. I see him shooting the shit with our teammates. I see him throwing back his head and balancing on one skate, shooting an imaginary arrow into the rafters to celebrate a goal.

He was my teammate.

He was my best friend.

When we finally arrive, the arena is locked down. That makes sense. The team is in Buffalo; they should be dropping the puck in half an hour.

I make my way around back to the player's parking lot. A single security guard is hunched in his booth, eyes lit by a flickering screen. He already has his window open by the time I roll up.

"Hey, Dwayne," I say, after lowering my own window.

"Mr. Rider," he says, standing a little straighter. "I'm sorry, sir. No one said you'd be coming in tonight."

"No problem," I say. "It was a last-minute decision."

"Jack and Bulldog are on duty up in the main booth," he says. "I'll let them know you're on your way."

"Thanks," I say. The guys will be keeping watch over two dozen security screens. If Dwayne puts them on notice, they won't have to leave their comfortable booth. "Quiet night tonight?"

"Just what you'd expect on Christmas Eve. Totally dead."

Totally dead.

"Have a good one," I say, and I roll up my window. When I park in the reserved spot closest to the door, my name looks like a mistake on the sign.

I start to walk around to open Aeryn's door, but she lets herself out. Her arms fold around her waist, like she's trying not to puke.

I punch in the security code at the door and wait for an answering buzz. The door feels heavy when I finally yank it open. "The layout's different from the last time you were here," I tell Aeryn. "We finished renovations three years ago."

"I've never been here," she says. Her voice sounds very small, like someone shrank her down to the size of a puck.

I start to protest—of course she's been here. But that's a lie.

She came to Atlantic City to visit her brother. She stayed to fuck me. Once she and I started…whatever the hell it was we started, she stayed as far away from the rink as she could. She didn't want Logan to know what we were doing. She didn't want to give anything away.

"Then let me show you around," I say, keeping my voice perfectly even. I own the Aces. I have keys to every door in the arena.

We start in my office—top floor, ocean view. There's my desk and two couches, a work table for hashing out contracts and chairs where I can argue with idiots who think they know the game better than I do. There are four televisions mounted on the wall, so I can watch multiple games at once. My private restroom comes with a shower and dressing room.

Downstairs, I start in on the official arena tour. There's the media gallery—TV and radio and press. I show her the refrigerator filled with pints of Aces Wild ice cream—a promotion with a local dairy that just keeps giving back.

We walk through the laundry and the kitchen and three different rooms filled with medical equipment. I show her our state-of-the-art gym. We stop by the visiting team's locker room —clean and organized, but stripped down to basic requirements.

The equipment room is next—a wonder of precision sporting gear. There are rows and rows of sweaters, every number in every design the team has worn this season. Entire battalions of pads fill shelves, and helmets line up like shiny boulders. A forest of sticks is broken out by player, so each man can have the weapon he prefers. Shelves of skates stretch on for miles.

We pass through to the Aces' locker room.

Her gaze goes past the metal benches, straight to Logan's locker. His sweater still hangs like he's starting tonight's game—number 23. His skates are polished, the blades newly sharpened. There's a photo of the team—the last one either of us played on—making the post-season for the first time in thirty-seven years. Without Logan and me, they went out in the first round. There's a photo of the Reardon family—Mickey and his five boys, with Aeryn on the end.

"What—?" she starts to ask, but gives up on the question.

"It's a memorial," I say. I don't tell her it was my first official order as owner of the team.

She swallows hard and nods.

I take her through the tunnel that leads to the bench. Almost all of the lights are off around the rink—just the red exit signs glow and a handful of security beacons. I could call down to Jack and Bulldog, ask them to turn on the overheads, but it's peaceful here in the gloom.

"It's huge," Aeryn says, her voice barely a whisper.

I nod. "The first time I practiced with the Aces, I'd just come up from New Brunswick, from the AHL team. I climbed over the boards and skated to center ice, and I thought someone had played some sort of practical joke. The ice looked bigger than the state of New Jersey."

She smiles politely, but I'm willing to bet she didn't hear a word I said. She's looking up in the rafters. She finds his number —23 again—on a flag as tall as two grown men.

"I retired it," I say. "The first year I owned the team."

Her eyes well up. She takes my hand. "Thank you," she says.

I shrug because I don't know how to respond. *You're welcome* implies I did a good thing, but I didn't. I did the only thing I could under the circumstances.

Her fingers tighten on mine. "I want to stand beneath it," she says. "Beside you. Come on. Let's get some skates."

"I don't skate."

"Please," she says, like that will make all the difference.

I shake my head.

She drops to her knees, right there, beside the boards. Tears glisten on her lashes as she looks up at me. "Please," she says again. "I'll never ask for anything else, Gage, not ever again. But we owe this to him. Tonight, on this anniversary, he deserves one last goodbye from both of us. Together." When I don't say anything, she grabs my hand. "*Gage,*" she pleads. "If not for him, then for me. I need you to put on those skates."

11

AERYN

For a moment, I think he'll walk away. He looks down the tunnel toward the locker room. His eyes shine in the dim light, and his face is drawn.

"I can't," he finally says.

"Can't?" I ask, squeezing his hand. "Or won't?"

He pulls his fingers out of my reach. "What difference does it make?"

I clamber to my feet. "He would have done it for you."

"Yeah. Right."

"He loved you."

"Right up until he landed an uppercut to my gut."

"That was my fault."

Gage's hands curl into knots as he glares at me. I can't remember ever seeing rage like this on his face. That's not who he is. But he sounds like a man trying to keep from putting his fist through a wall when he says, "It was never your fault."

"*Our* fault, then. Both of us."

He shakes his head, one tight twist.

I set my palm against his jaw. It feels like it's about to crumble, like a suspension bridge is collapsing. "Both of us," I repeat. "That's why I need you with me, out there on the ice."

He brushes away my hand with a barely capped energy. I know he could have broken my wrist. He could have shoved me over the boards, onto the rink. Even in his fury, in his misery, he's doing his best to protect me.

"Gage... Help me say goodbye."

"It's been ten fucking years."

"Then it's time we're both set free."

"Free?" He says the word like he's never heard it before. "What makes you think I deserve to be *free*?"

"He wouldn't want you to—"

"You don't know that!" Gage's shout bounces off the rafters.

"He was my brother." My voice shakes.

"And he was my best friend! He's dead! I let him die! And if you think strapping on some skates and standing beneath a goddamn teal-and-white banner can change any of that, you're out of your fucking mind."

He stomps down the tunnel like he's just been given a five-minute major for fighting. I take three steps after him before I pull myself up short. He's bellowing in the locker room, *keening*, like someone is pulling his heart through his ribcage.

There's a crash, and I realize he must have thrown one of the benches against a wall of lockers. There's a pounding like someone's trying to open the gates of hell; a fist on metal, over and over again, hard enough to bruise, to break bones. There's a clatter I can't begin to parse and then that bellowing again, half shout, half moan, like a monster is dying.

And then, silence.

My pulse is loud in my ears, and my breath comes in short, sharp gasps. My fingertips tingle, and I realize I'm getting dizzy, so I sink onto the bench.

This is where Logan sat during games. Gage, too. This is

where they watched their teammates on the ice, where they taunted their enemies. This is where they joked and spit and swore. Where they became brothers.

And then it ended—just like *that*.

I close my eyes, and I'm back on Beach Avenue.

Logan left for the rink fifteen minutes ago, giving himself extra time in case the Christmas Eve traffic is bad. Gage is running late because I hid his car keys. I tell him I'll give them back after he makes me come three times.

He doesn't throw me over his shoulder and drag me to his room. He doesn't gag me either. We're alone in the house. No one can hear.

He just sits on the sagging couch, knees spread wide, and he drags me onto his lap. He flips my skirt over my arse and yanks my knickers down to my knees. His strokes are hard and fast. He promises twenty, but he only gets to twelve before he slips three fingers between my soaked folds.

I scream his name as I come around his hand and he laughs, saying "That's one." I'm writhing on his lap, my red arse high in the air as I beg-not-beg him to spare me my last eight strokes, when the front door slams back on its hinges.

Logan's come back for the phone he forgot on the coffee table.

My brother yanks my arm hard enough to make me yelp, throwing me halfway across the room. Gage is on his feet before I steady myself against the wall. I pull up my knickers and try to straighten my skirt. "Easy, bruh," Gage says, holding his hands out from his sides.

The room smells like sex.

"What the *fuck* are you doing to my sister?" Logan hollers.

"It's okay," I say.

"Shut up, Aeryn." Logan circles for an opening, not taking his eyes off Gage.

"Don't tell her to shut up," Gage says.

"She's my sister, gobshite. I can tell her anything I want."

"Logan," I say, trying to get the truth out before this gets any worse. "It's okay. I—"

Logan cuts me off by snarling at Gage. "She's not one of your whores, shitehawk. She's a goddamn Reardon."

My cheeks flush with anger. All my life, my brothers have treated me like I'm their property. Reardon this. Reardon that. But I'm my own feckin' person.

I grab Logan's arm to make him pay attention to me. "I consented, arsehole. I wanted him to do it."

My brother glares at me with disgust. "Yeah, sure. You wanted him to spank you raw."

I nod. It's mortifying to admit the truth, but I'll do it to keep the two of them from fighting. I send a pleading glance to Gage, praying he'll let me make this right. "I did."

"Holy Christ…" Logan whirls back to Gage. "How long have you been beating my sister?"

I shout before Gage can answer. "It isn't *beating*."

Logan snorts. "Fine." His tone twists into something mocking, something that sounds insanely polite. "Let's start with this, then. Excuse me, Mr. Dry Shite. How long have you been fucking my little sister?"

Gage swings first. I scream as Logan blocks his fist with a forearm. Before either of them can throw another punch, I shout, "Since Thanksgiving! We've been seeing each other since Thanksgiving! I didn't want you to find out this way. We were going to tell you before New Year's, before I head back to school. I promise."

Logan is staring at me like I just told him we murder babies in the kitchen. "Where the fuck have you been staying?"

I look around wildly. "Here," I say. Then, like I owe him an explanation: "You were on your road trip for two weeks."

"And after we got home?"

I shrug helplessly. I don't want to tell him about all the times I huddled in Gage's shower, waiting for Logan to head out to practice or a game. He doesn't need to know I spent an entire night in Gage's closet when the rookies were here for pizza, because I was afraid some drunk newbie wouldn't wait his turn to piss in the jacks down the hall. "Here."

Logan scowls. "Here? And I didn't have a clue?"

"We were quiet," I try to explain.

"What did you do?" Logan snarls at Gage. "Gag her?"

Neither of us answers. Logan's face flushes crimson. "You *gagged* my little sister?"

"I—" I try to explain.

"You motherfucking, cocksucking *cunt!*"

Logan's knuckles split Gage's lip. Gage fires back, pummeling my brother's torso. Logan grabs his hair and kicks at the back of his knee, and they land like elephants in a waterhole.

This isn't a hockey fight. This isn't slipping and sliding on the ice, landing a few sharp punches before a ref pulls them apart.

This is two grown men, doing their level best to kill each other.

"Stop it!" I scream. "Logan! Gage! Goddammit, both of you!"

I see a chance and I seize it, diving between the pair of them. I throw myself across Gage's chest, flinging my arms wide to block Logan's next blow.

My brother cocks his arm and aims his bloody knuckles. "Get out of the way, Aeryn."

I'm breathing too hard to choke out a word.

"Get out o' the fuckin' way," Logan growls.

Gage is struggling beneath me. He's winded. Logan's done some damage.

"Jesus Christ," Logan finally swears. "The pair o' ya deserve each other."

He turns on his heel, staggering a couple of steps before he regains his balance. Swiping a hand over the coffee table, he comes up with his phone. He sneers at me from the door. "Get your arse out of here by the time I get home tonight, or I'll tell Da."

Logan slams the door hard enough to crack the glass in its window. I roll off Gage. He lies there for a minute, breathing like a stallion. He groans when he lurches to his feet.

"I'll drive you to the train station," he says.

"I'm not going anywhere."

"Just until your brother cools off. We play New York on New Year's Day. You and I can talk to him after the game."

"I'm not leaving."

"He doesn't make idle threats. When he goes to your father—"

"I'll tell Da I'm a grown woman. I get to make my own choices. This isn't South Side business. You don't have to be afraid."

"Jesus, babygirl," Gage sighs. "I'm not afraid. I want to do what's right for you."

"Staying is right."

He shakes his head. But then he looks at his watch. "I have to get to the game. We'll talk about this when I get home."

"You can talk. But I'm not leaving."

"Fine," he says, but he doesn't believe me.

"Fine," I say.

He shuts the door more carefully than Logan.

I straighten the room. I move my toothbrush from its hiding place in the nightstand to the bathroom counter. I shift my box of Barry's Gold from Gage's top dresser drawer to the kitchen, right beside the electric kettle.

I'm eating a bowl of corn flakes when the puck drops. Players on both teams are chippy; Boston injured the Aces' goalie when they played just ten days ago. The Aces' center goes down in the crease, tripped by a Boston stick between his legs. Logan's gloves are off before the whistle blows.

For a minute, it's just a typical hockey fight. The men square up, Boston and Atlantic City. Gage is late getting to the scrum;

he's favoring his right knee. A Boston defenseman sucker-punches him, and Gage's head lashes back. He crashes to the ice, sliding halfway to the blue line.

No one notices. No one cares.

Because Logan is lying on the bright blue ice in front of the crease. He's staring up at the rafters like he's looking on the face of God. His throat is slashed; someone's skate has carved him an extra smile.

Players on both teams wave for help from the bench. Two Aces skate over to the boards, ferrying a trainer onto the ice. White towels bloom with red, only to be replace by more cloth. More.

Gage struggles to his knees, trailing one hand on the ice to keep his balance. He tries to drag himself to Logan's side, but his coordination is shot. He sprawls like a kid in a snowsuit.

He's still trying to reach the goal when Logan dies.

12

GAGE

F uck.

I sweep a pile of goalie pads off a shelf, sending the teal-and-purple equipment flying. I knew tonight was a fucking mistake, the instant Aeryn suggested it. Every mile of that silent drive down from New York proved I was right. I should have pulled over before we passed New Brunswick.

We could have gone to a bar there, one of the dives Logan and I went to when we were in the AHL. Drink a toast. Share some stories. I could have had her home before midnight.

Not that "home" makes any difference. She's been up-front since I saw her at the bar in Kynk's Great Room. She's flying back to Chicago tomorrow morning. She's a Reardon, through and through.

Get your arse out of here by the time I get home tonight, or I'll tell Da.

I can still hear Logan's voice, rough with the Irish accent that only came out when he fought. I remember every word he said in that shithole house on Beach Avenue.

She's not one of your whores, shitehawk.
How long have you been beating my sister?
You motherfucking, cocksucking cunt!

I crash into a pile of hockey sticks and send them flying. Logan wasn't a fucking Boy Scout. He had his pick of the puck bunnies. More than once, he took two girls back to his hotel room at the same time. He paid a thousand bucks to a one-night-stand who said he knocked her up, then ten thousand more to keep her from telling the Atlantic City Press about the abortion. Every man on the team knew he was the reason the trainers started leaving a big glass bowl of rubbers on the counter in the treatment room.

But in all the years we played together, I never heard about him hitting a woman—whether she wanted it or not. The place we planned to build in the abandoned Brooklyn subway tunnel was a sports bar, not a sex club. Logan knew sports. That's what he wanted.

I pick up the closest stick and beat it against the floor of the equipment room. One blow. Two. Three. The blade snaps off, and I grab myself another. It breaks on the first hit. Fucking loser. I kick the rest of the sticks like they're kindling.

Yeah, Logan wanted a sports bar. But I'm the sick mother-fucker who started Kynk.

At first, I did it because I didn't want hockey players drop-ping by. I didn't want to be reminded that *I* was the reason Logan died.

If we hadn't fought on in the house on Beach, he would have been in better shape for the game. A few seconds faster. More flexible. Able to dodge.

If I had caught the puck on my stick and taken it down ice, no one would have fought at the game. Or we would have fought later, without the freak slash of that blade.

If I had seen that sucker punch, I wouldn't have been concussed. I could have gotten to him before the trainer. Put pressure on the wound. Kept him from bleeding out.

If, if, if… A fraction of a second here, a quarter of an inch there, anything would have made a difference. There were a million ways I could have saved him. One fucking path that let him die.

I stumble against a shelf of gloves, new ones, stiff. I throw one against the wall with all my strength, feeling the tendons torque in my elbow. A professional athlete would take care not to wreck his arm. I'm no athlete anymore. I'm just an owner.

I throw three more gloves, then knock down a rack of helmets.

I *can't* go on that ice. I can't skate with Aeryn like some lovesick kid. I can't pretend that Logan's blood hasn't seeped into the fucking foundation of Aces Arena.

He's the reason I bought the team, instead of playing until I was too old to lace up skates. He's the reason I run Kynk, instead of a sports bar where all our friends could hang around and shoot the shit. He's the reason I should have walked away from Aeryn at the Great Room bar, and he's the reason I took her home, and he's the reason I'll never get to have her again.

I roar like a bull and head back to destroy the Aces' skates on their goddamn, fucking shelves.

13

AERYN

For the first time since I met Gage Rider fifteen years ago, I don't know who the hell he is.

When Logan called us from the draft to say he'd been chosen by the Aces, he put Gage on the phone, saying, "They're taking Rider too! Say hello to Gage!" I said, "Hello, Gage," and that felt right.

When Logan bought out the first row at center ice for their debut game in the NHL—both rookies called up on the same day—he dragged Gage over to the glass before the game and shouted, "Wish us luck!" I wished them luck, and that was right too.

When Logan and Gage moved into the Beach Avenue house, Da ordered me to come down from New York, telling me to set up a kitchen for "the boys" and make them their first meal. I asked Gage his favorite, and I made lasagna instead of Granny's lamb stew, which is what Logan would have named— another thing so right I never thought to question my decision.

I flirted with Gage every time I came to visit.

I took him up on his offer, when he caught me with my hand down my pants.

I stayed in Atlantic City for all of winter break, instead of heading back to my apartment and my classmates and my life in New York.

I let him tie me up. Gag me. Blindfold me. Break me and put me back together and leave me begging for more, more, more.

All those things were *right.* They were what I wanted. What I needed. How I fit Gage Rider into my life.

But I don't know what to do with the man who just raged into the locker room now. I don't know how to reach him. How to keep him.

It seems like such a simple thing: Skate with me to the center of the ice. He put on his first skates when he was three. There's a room filled with equipment back there; there must be forty pairs just his size. He's fit. He's capable. God knows he has the stamina of a firefighter.

But he won't do it.

Can't do it?

It doesn't matter anymore.

I turn my back on the rink and make my way down the tunnel.

The locker room looks like a tornado swept through. Three benches stand on end, leaning against walls where someone—Gage—threw them. A floor-to-ceiling mirror is destroyed, a star of shattered glass bursting from the center, slammed by Gage's fist or his head or one of the benches he tossed. The announcements on the team bulletin board are shredded into confetti.

None of that matters.

What matters is the locker in the middle of the wall. The trampled sweater with the number 23. The broken shelf, hanging by one bent nail. The skates collapsed like burst balloons, blades buried in the floor.

The photos look like they've been thrown against the wall. Both frames are shattered. The team pic is bent almost in half.

It's just *stuff*. Nothing that matters. Logan isn't buried here. His memory will live on, even without the locker-room shrine.

But his ruined locker tells me what I need to do. It's time to go back to Chicago. To forget about Atlantic City, about New York, about Gallagher Samson and restaurants and Kynk. That part of my life is over now. Forever.

I'm Aeryn Reardon. It's time for me to go home.

I sink onto the one bench still standing in its proper place.

Da's pilot is supposed to fetch me from Teterboro before dawn tomorrow. I might as well call him now. Tell him to file new flight plans. Fly me from Atlantic City to home. He can do it tonight, and we'll both have all of Christmas Day with our families.

My phone feels too heavy in my hand, like someone swapped my usual mobile for a lead brick. I stare at the screen for longer than I should. It takes forever for me to remember that I correspond with the pilot by text; that's how we schedule our travel.

I pull up the last message I sent, confirming my plans for tomorrow. I tap the number, then the bright blue icon that launches a call.

One ring.

Two.

It's Christmas Eve; we must be getting close to midnight. Of course the pilot isn't answering.

Three rings.

A fourth.

Voicemail picks up, and I swallow before I start my message. "My plans have changed, and I'm heading back to Chicago as soon as possible. But I'm no longer leaving from New York. I'm heading back from—"

"Aeryn."

It's Gage's voice, behind me. I choke off my message to the pilot.

"Hang up," Gage says.

My phone feels frozen in my hand.

"You can call him back in a minute," Gage says. "Just let me say something first. Please…"

He circles the bench like he's crossing a minefield to stand in front of me. As my fingers start to tremble, Gage Rider sinks to his knees.

14

GAGE

I take her phone out of her hand, tapping the screen to end her call. I place it on the bench beside her, close enough that she can grab it if she wants to. She needs to know she has options. She's the one in control.

Her hands are shaking like she's soaking in an ice bath after a particularly brutal game. I take them between mine, wishing I could fill her with comfort as easily as I transfer warmth.

"Aeryn," I say, to make her look at me.

She doesn't want to. She stares at the mirror I broke when I threw the bench across the room. She frowns when she spies a bit of wood that broke off one of Logan's picture frames. She closes her eyes as I wait.

"Aeryn," I say again. "I fucked up everything. It's all my fault."

Because that's the truth. After my tantrum, after tearing apart the locker room, the equipment room, my fragile hold on my temper, I've plummeted to the bottom line.

I fucked up.

Ten years ago.

Tonight.

All of this is on me. And looking at the wreckage of my life, I can only pray it isn't too late to convince Aeryn to forgive me.

Her sigh is so exhausted I want to gather her close to my chest, to swaddle her in flannel, to wrap her in down comforters. I want to keep her whole and safe and comfortable forever.

"I was there, too," she finally says. "Not at the feckin' game —that was just an accident. But I was on Beach Avenue for the entire month. I was the eejit who chose to hide."

"I didn't want to lose a single minute with you," I say. "I didn't want anyone stealing your attention. I wanted to be the only man in the world who saw you, first thing every morning and last thing every night."

"It was all so new," she says with a soft, tiny smile. "So exciting. You made me feel things I'd never felt before—physical things, yeah, but *heart* things, too. You changed me, Gage Rider. You made me fall in love."

She's a million times braver than I am.

"No, babygirl," I finally say. "*You* changed *me*. I didn't even know what was happening at first. I thought you were just another girl. Just Logan's kid sister. Fun. Funny. But not…"

I know precisely how much I can bench press and how much I can dead lift and how fast I can run on a fucking treadmill. But I don't have a clue how to do the one thing I need to do right now. How to say the one word she most needs to hear.

But she said it. So I can too.

"I love you," I say. And when she doesn't pull back, I say it again. "I love you, and I always have. Despite all the things we did wrong. Maybe because of them. Because of all the time we've spent apart. All the ways we miss him. Logan."

"We would have explained it all to him," she says, her Irish lilt turning her words into a poem. "Made him understand who we really are. What we want. What we need. I love you because you were there that last day. I love you because you fought for me. I love you because he would have forgiven the pair of us, if he'd had half a chance, if he'd just had time to get over his surprise."

She's a million times smarter than I am too.

I could never put the words together the way she just has. I couldn't make them flow right. Couldn't make them sing.

But the rightness of every syllable she's said settles into my bones. I love her. She loves me. And all the choices we make together, all the things we do, make us stronger, as individuals and as a pair. *That's* the bond that holds us together—man and woman, Dom and sub.

Love.

Trust.

Truth.

"Come here," I say, rising to my feet and taking her by the hand. She moves willingly, following me out of the locker room.

But when she sees the mess I've made of all the team's equipment, she gasps. "Gage!"

I manage a rueful grin. "What good is owning a team, if you can't tear things apart every once in a while?" I glance at the destruction. "My equipment managers just earned triple holiday bonuses."

"You can't buy your way out of everything," she chides.

I look directly in her eyes. "I know. I promise. I know."

I wait for her to nod before I make my way to the shelves of jet-black skates. They're made for men, for warriors who need protection from flying pucks and slashing sticks. But a few of those men have smaller feet than average. A seven in these boots will match her women's nine. I snag a pair of heavy socks, for good measure.

I hold the skates like a bouquet, as if I can buy her back with steel and leather. The laces spill from my hands like trailing ivy. "Please," I say. "Sit." I nod toward a bench I didn't manage to move.

She swallows hard. But she sits.

I kneel before her for the second time tonight. I tug at the skate, loosening the tongue and shoving the laces out of the way. I take her left ankle in my hand like I'm collecting a crystal goblet, and when I slip off her stiletto, I can't help myself. I bend down to kiss the arch of her foot.

Her toes curl, and we both laugh as I help her into a sock before planting her heel inside the skate. My fingers tug the laces, automatically cinching them tight to give her the support she'll need. The cords are long; I wrap them around the top of the boot twice before double-knotting a bow.

"You're good at this," she says, eyeing me through her lashes.

"Lots and lots of practice," I say, making short work of the second sock and skate.

She watches as I move down the shelf, finding a pair of size thirteens for myself. I'm walloped by a flash of memory as I toe off my shoes. I can't count the number of times I've pulled on hockey skates—playing for the Aces, for Dartmouth, for Brighton Academy. All the pick-up games, all the special coaching sessions, all the lessons, just hitting the ice for fun.

Ten years I've gone without. Ten years I've forbidden myself the essential, basic pleasure of my first boyish love—hockey. Ten years I've stayed away.

Maybe I thought lightning would strike me. My feet would burst into flames. Logan's ghost would rise up to choke me, dragging me off to hell.

They're just skates. I'm simply going to glide across a sheet of ice, with a fearless, beautiful woman by my side.

Our blades are covered with plastic guards to make walking easier and to protect the sharp metal. I find my balance immediately—this is easier than riding a bike, more basic than sex.

Aeryn, though, wobbles. "The boots are so rigid!" she says.

"You'll get used to it. Don't forget—you don't have a toe pick."

She looks down at her feet like she's having second thoughts. But she lets me take her hand. She allows me to walk her through the locker room and down the tunnel to the ice illuminated by exit signs and security lights.

Gripping the boards, she lets me pull away her plastic guards, left foot first, then right. I drop mine beside hers, and we both step onto the rink.

She wavers again, flailing her arms for balance. I catch her around the waist before she gets close to falling. "Easy, babygirl," I say, breathing in the scent of my shampoo on her hair.

Her laugh is shaky, so I lace my fingers between hers. We push off together, matching stroke for stroke as we make our way down the long side of the rink.

My muscles still know how to glide. But the air feels colder than I remember, pressing in from the shadows. The sound of the slicing blades is sharper, the hiss louder than I expect.

We take a full lap around the rink, holding hands. Then Aeryn slips her fingers from mine. She lengthens her stride, picking up her pace. She rides out each stroke to its limit, gliding into a wide, sweeping turn.

She knows better than to try jumping—she'd need a toe pick for that. She doesn't even try a spin. Instead, she pushes for pure, unbridled speed.

I stay close enough to hear her laughter, but I let her take the lead. When she begins her turn at the end, I cut across the rink, gliding backward as she hurtles toward me. We make another loop like that—giving and taking, matching each other, dancing on the ice.

She's breathing hard now. Her strokes are coming slower. She catches herself at the end of the rink, pushing up against the goal. It shudders as it takes her weight, but she doesn't have enough momentum to knock it off its posts. I come to a stop beside her, sending up a spray of ice.

Her hands are tight on the goal. She's looking down at the

blue-tinted ice beneath her feet, at the semi-circle that marks the crease.

"This is where it happened."

She doesn't phrase it as a question, but I answer anyway. "Yes."

"In less than five minutes."

"Yes."

"He must have been so afraid."

I don't have an answer for that. I've thought about it hundreds of times. But I'm not holding back from Aeryn anymore. "He would have gone into shock almost immediately. But he could see the trainers he trusted. They'd patched him up dozens of times before. He would have trusted them to do it again."

"I wish I'd been here."

Even if she'd come to the game, she would have been on the other side of the glass. She couldn't have reached him in time. I say, "That was *my* job. *I* was supposed to be here, holding his hand, telling him he'd make it through, promising to tell his family he loved them."

"He knew all that."

"Did he?"

"He was a Reardon. He knew his clan." Her voice is suddenly thicker with Irish than I've ever heard it before. "He knew his friends too. He forgave ya before he died."

"You don't know that."

"I do. Because I'm a Reardon, too."

She's a girl. And the youngest. And Logan didn't seem inclined to accept that she wanted to be a sub—much less with his best friend as her Dom. But she needs to believe her story. She needs to think it's true. So I say, "He forgave both of us."

She offers me a smile—simple and pure. Her eyes are huge in the dim light. Her hair gleams red.

Graceful as some sort of sea creature, she sinks to her knees. She touches her fingertips to her lips, then brushes them across the blue ice. I don't know if she says a prayer when she bows her head or if she's only whispering a final farewell.

I hook a hand around her biceps when she starts to rise to her feet. She overbalances a little, leaning into my chest. Folding my arm around her waist, I skate us over to the bench and match the plastic guards to her blades. She lets me help her down the tunnel to the ransacked equipment room.

The place looks worse than when we left it. It occurs to me that I should be ashamed of what I've done, but I won't waste a second on that. I didn't hurt anyone else. I didn't hurt myself.

And for the first time in a decade, I feel like I can truly breathe.

Back to my knees in front of her, I strip my double knots from her laces. I tug off the skates, then the socks, setting everything aside before I take care of my own boots.

It's time to return to the real world. I have to drive us back to New York. She needs to fly home to Chicago in the morning.

Before I can stand, though, she reaches out one steady hand, settling it in the center of my chest. My heart rate doubles, igniting an invisible spark between us. She feels it, I know, because her lips curve into a smile.

"Thank you," she says. "For bringing me here. For taking me out on the ice."

I want to grab on to the electricity sizzling between us. I want to tell her it was nothing, but that isn't true. It was almost more than I could handle.

You're welcome isn't enough. Thanking her in return would almost hit the mark, but that isn't right either.

She takes away my decision before I settle on a response. Flattening her palm against my chest, she leans forward to press her lips against mine. The spark between us flares into something bigger, something that burns off all the oxygen in the room.

"Let me do something for *you* now," she whispers. "*Sir.*"

15

AERYN

His fingers close around my wrist, holding my hand over his heart. His gaze comes to a sudden boil, pouring off heat as he studies my face.

"You don't have to do this," he says. "We can take things more slowly."

"We've had ten years of slow. I want this. I want you. Tonight."

He brushes my hair off my face. "*Tiramisu*, if things get too rough."

"Cranberry tart," I say. "All night long. Take me to your office. Please."

A wicked light flares in his eyes. "We won't get that far, babygirl."

His kiss is danger and desire, longing and sin, his tongue challenging mine for control. His teeth catch my lower lip, closing hard enough to make me moan. He growls when he frees me: "On your feet, babygirl."

Gripping my elbow with one hand, he edges me toward the door. He snags a couple of hockey sticks from a dense tangle before he marches me into the treatment room.

It's a large space, part sterile medical office, part high-tech spa, part professional-grade gymnasium. A counter stretches along one wall, with cabinets above and below. The opposing wall is filled with gear—crutches hanging on hooks, braces for every part of the body, support belts and weighted vests and equipment bags. A treadmill hulks beside an elliptical. A lightbox on the wall waits to display X-rays. A hip-deep tub sits beneath a heavy plastic cover in one corner, next to an industrial-size ice-making machine.

This is the opposite of Kynk. At the club, everything was designed to signal sensual decadence, with an undercurrent of wealth. This treatment room is a place of business. Everything is cold. Unemotional. This is where men come to be healed.

"Strip," Gage says.

My arms automatically cross my chest, startled into defense by his harsh tone. Something twists inside me, a viper of warning. He said we should take things more slowly, and I didn't believe him. Now I'll pay for my over-confidence.

"This isn't a good beginning, babygirl," he warns. "Don't make me repeat myself."

I swallow hard, trying to master the roller-coaster swoop in my belly. When that doesn't help, I close my eyes, bending to capture the hem of my knit dress.

"Eyes on me, babygirl," he says. "You don't get to slip away like that."

I take a steadying breath while my face is hidden by the dress. I toss my hair as soon as my head is free. My fingers clutch the soft wool to my chest as if I can hide my mis-matched lingerie, the rose-studded black lace bra I wore to seduce Gage at the club and the simple cotton knickers Martha Gallagher provided.

"Drop it," Gage commands, nodding toward my dress.

He sounds like he's ordering a dog to give up a tennis ball. Before I can think about consequences, I say, "Woof."

He's faster than a lightning bolt, closing the distance between us. His fingers clamp on either side of my jaw, pulling my head to a sharp angle. Heat radiates off his body, sizzling my flank. "Drop. It."

My fingers tremble as I release the sweater.

"Kneel," he says, emphasizing the order by pointing with his free hand.

I drop to the floor.

My body remembers the rules. I sit back on my heels, my thighs spread. My spine is as straight as a hockey stick, my head perfectly level. The backs of my hands rest on my thighs, palms open in a gesture of absolute surrender.

I don't understand why I need this, why I crave Gage's commands. I'm a rebel by nature. When Da tells me anything, I parse his words to carve out every possible exception. My brothers know the quickest way to make me freeze is to order me to move. My teachers at culinary school despaired of my ever mastering the five mother sauces of French cooking; I was too intent on making my own variations.

But here, now, between us, Gage's word is law.

Maybe it's because he was my first. Maybe it's because we needed to work together to hide our relationship from Logan. Maybe it's because he's built an empire reading reactions—on the ice, in the boardroom, at the club.

Whatever the cause, something inside me is tuned to Gage's frequency. He pulls me like the North Pole draws a compass. He perfects me.

"Stay," he says

I watch him hungrily as he crosses the room, only my eyes moving so I don't break posture. He takes his time, pulling his shirt from the waistband of his jeans. He works the buttons at each wrist, folding back his cuffs with a precision that drags a whine from my throat.

"Not yet, babygirl," he says, chuckling as he pulls the shirt over his head. His belt is next, whispering through the loops on his jeans.

I want him to drape it around my neck and cinch it tight. I want him to flick the end against my pebbled nipples. I want... I lick my lips, fighting the urge to raise my hands.

"Stay..." He draws out the reminder as he steps out of his jeans, snagging silk boxers and socks with the same smooth maneuver.

Ten years out of the game, he still has an athlete's body—broad shoulders, narrow hips, muscles sculpted like a statue of a Greek god. His cock is thicker than I remember. When his hands flex by his hips, something flips deep inside me, a switch he installed years ago.

"Please," I beg.

"Not yet, babygirl. Not for a long, long time."

I can't help myself. I need to feel that velvet-covered steel. Rocking forward on my knees, I stretch to touch him, to taste him.

He pounces. For a moment, there's a struggle. I'm frantic to prove that I can make him happy. His fingers close around one of my wrists, but he's close enough that I can guide his cock to my mouth. He's grappling for my other hand, though, the one that's tight around him. When he squeezes the small bones of my wrist, I have no choice but to let him go.

As my lips slip off his reddened tip, I howl my defeat. "Let me do this, ya feckin' shitehawk. Let me make you feel good."

"Oh, you'll do that, babygirl." He grunts as he drags me to my feet. "But not until *I* say."

He pulls me toward the wall filled with cabinets. Holding both of my wrists with one uncompromising hand, he scrambles for one of the hockey sticks he left on the counter. Settling my belly against the lower cabinet, he holds me in place with his weight against my back.

His cock presses against my arse. If I wasn't wearing knickers, I could spread my legs and shift my hips. Push against him until he fills my needy core.

But I *am* wearing knickers. And he's bigger than I am. Stronger than I can ever hope to be. He fumbles for something in the cabinet beside my head, swearing as I shift under him.

It only takes him a moment to find what he needs and then he shifts his weight, pinning me with one carved hip. There's a scream like an animal dying, but it isn't coming from me. I realize he's ripping athletic tape off a roll, wrapping thick white strips around my wrist, then around the hockey stick.

He binds my right wrist to the wooden shaft, then shifts his attention to my left arm. It's awkward with the stick above my head. He positions my wrist nearly at the end, by the blade, cementing my grip with a dozen rounds of tape. He stops just short of dislocating my shoulders.

Before I can figure out the new weight of the stick, he snaps the clasp on my black lace bra. Reaching around from behind, he frees my right breast first, pinching the stony nipple hard enough to make me yip.

My bound hands are useless. I have no defense as he savages my left breast too. I howl as arrows of pure sensation shoot straight to my clit.

Caging my body with his, he gathers my hair off my heated neck. I lean forward from my waist, letting the cabinets take the weight of the stick and my arms. Gage moves with me, finding the pulse point beneath my jaw with his mouth. He sucks for a moment, which almost feels like comfort. Before I can relax, though, he starts to tongue my throat.

Every nerve ending in my body is tossed into a bonfire. I need to pull away, and I can't, and the tension tightens the muscles of my thighs. He quickens his pace, licking, lashing, tearing me apart.

It's so simple, what he's doing, and so completely devastating. My fingers splay on the cabinet like broken branches. I'm balancing on my tiptoes, desperate for release. I'm moaning every time I pant, so close, so very close, almost, almost there.

He stops.

"You goddamn, fucking shitehawk," I start, the second I get enough breath to speak.

"Language, babygirl," he says.

"How's *this* for language? Let me come, you motherf—"

I don't know where he got the scissors—on the counter, or in a cabinet, maybe from one of the drawers. The cold steel against my right hip makes me shudder, convulsing almost double at the shock. I jerk back from the cabinet, unsteady with my arms above my head. Before I can find my balance, he snips again, pressing against my left hip.

Taking my knickers from behind, he tugs toward the small of my back. The cloth is soft enough to glide through the slickness of my soaked folds, but it's rough enough to push my throbbing clit to the very edge.

If there was more fabric, if he held the pressure longer, if he went back to his ravaging assault on my neck, I could come. Instead, he strands me on the very edge of release again.

"Just do it!" I scream, when I realize he's left me hanging. "Fuck me or—"

He fills my mouth with cotton.

My knickers are already drenched, coating my tongue with honey and salt. I push with my tongue, trying to spit them out, but Gage is ready for that too. He doesn't use tape this time. Instead, he grabs an elastic bandage, the type meant for splinting and sprains. It feels like sponge against my cheeks, pulling tighter with every round.

I try to buck him off, but he has all the advantage. I'm trussed up with the hockey stick, breasts bare, mouth so full I have to concentrate to breathe. But none of that keeps me from screaming my protest, even as he presses another bandage into my hand.

I try to throw the roll at him, angling behind my head, but

he easily side-steps my attack. He retrieves the bandage and curls my fingers around it, squeezing firmly. "That's your safe-word now. Drop it if you want this game to stop."

Game.

I'm humiliated here—bare arse, bare breasts, arms stretched wide on the stick above my head. He's brought me to the edge twice and left me dangling. He's in charge of everything, in absolute control. He owns me.

And I have never been more turned on in my life.

I bow my head as best I can beneath the hockey stick, submitting.

He settles down to serious business then. He orders me to spread my legs, and when I don't move quickly enough, he positions them with his own rough hands. He collects the other hockey stick, the one I foolishly forgot. He lashes my ankles to the wood, same as my hands, setting my feet further apart than I think I can bear.

While he's down there, he bites my arse—not enough to draw blood, but enough to make me squeal into my knickers. He kisses the flaming mark he leaves behind, soothing with his lips first, then his tongue. As I press back into his face, his arm wraps around my hip. He finds my clit and reduces me to wordless pleading in seconds.

But still he doesn't let me come. Instead, he throws me over his shoulder like I'm some crazy bendable doll. He carries me over to one of the massage tables and puts me on my back

The table takes the weight of the stick in my hands, easing the pressure on my shoulders. His fingers close around my waist, dragging my arse toward the end of the table, until I feel the edge just behind my knees. He strokes my thighs, then, saying, "That's right, babygirl. Relax."

I'd scream if I thought it would do me any good. I can't relax with my arms stretched over my head. I can't relax with my feet strapped to a hockey stick, dangling beneath the table. I can't relax with my knees spread wide, displaying my most private parts like a filthy invitation.

Gage has seen every inch of my body. He's smelled me. Tasted me. But it's still reflex for my knees to close, for me to hide from his burning gaze.

He hasn't left me any room to maneuver. My feet are tied too far apart. I can't pull away in shame. I'm forced to lie here, belly rising and falling like I'm a wild animal in a trap.

But I'm still holding my roll of adhesive bandage. I'm clutching it tight, against even the faintest possibility of it slipping out of my grasp. I'm dirty and I'm desperate and I don't ever want this game to end.

Gage catches a rolling stool with his toes, pulling it over to the foot of the table. Straddling the feckin' seat, he settles between my legs. I groan as he pulls closer, unable to stop him, unable to wait.

He hits a switch on the end of the table, and the surface lowers so I'm even with his mouth. "Finally, babygirl," he says. "I've been dreaming of this for years."

16

GAGE

She's spread out before me, stretched, helpless. Her rib-cage rises and falls like she's been skating lines for hours. Heat ripples from the tangle of her pubes, carrying the sea-salt scent of her pussy.

She moans when I slip in one finger. She's wet, soaked, and she clenches her muscles around me, pulling me deeper.

She's been so good, taking her punishment. She deserves a reward. She's my babygirl, and I'm the only man who can tame her.

I add a second finger, pumping slowly, with a tap of my thumb to her clit each time the web of my hand settles home. She's chanting something behind her gag—I think it's *more, more, more.*

My babygirl is greedy, but I'm the one who wins. I add a third finger, curling at the end of each thrust, scraping at the tightest bundle of nerves inside her hot, slick hole.

Her hips rock off the table. Her feet flex above the stick. Her ribcage freezes as she holds her breath, as she wills me to free her, as she waits for sweet release.

I pull my hand away.

Her scream would break a lesser man.

She wants me. She needs me. But she's running far too hot. I need her to hold on for a few more minutes.

I roll the stool back in case she tries to catch me with the stick between her feet. I only have to take six steps to reach the ice bath. The stainless steel monster beside it sends out a steady hum. When I slide back the door, I find a waiting mountain of ice.

I scoop a handful of cubes into a plastic bin kept there for just that purpose. Well, maybe not that *exact* purpose—I remember long nights spent icing sprained fingers, others when a trainer wrapped packs around my aching joints after particularly brutal games.

Aeryn is lying still on the table when I return. Her breathing has slowed to something deep and steady. She's staring at the ceiling like she's reciting recipes to herself, or maybe trying out a prayer.

Her fingers are still knotted tight around the bandage.

I settle on my stool again, rolling back between her legs. This time, I go straight for her clit, sucking, licking, scraping with my teeth. She writhes above me, and now I think she's saying my name—*Gage, Gage, Gage*—begging.

She's primed after all the other teasing, ready to go off in less than a minute. One last lick is all she needs to finally set her free.

I slip a cube of ice inside her.

She screeches at the cold, her ass rising off the table. I stand between her legs, setting one chilled hand across her belly, retrieving more ice with the other.

I trace her nipples, which I didn't think could get any darker, any harder. I was wrong. I trail a melting cube across the furnace of her throat. I palm her mound, letting a handful of ice melt into her pubes.

When she's cool enough, calmed enough, I cross the room and retrieve one last thing from a bowl on the counter. Her eyes are closed when I get back to the table.

She's sobbing now, gasping into her panties, tears streaming into the halo of her hair. Her bra is pushed up under her chin. Her arms stretch over her head, sagging now, as if she's given up.

But she still holds the bandage.

"Babygirl," I say.

She lies there.

"Look at me, babygirl."

Her eyes flutter open. She looks dazed. Confused.

But she watches as I rip open the condom's foil packet. The fingers on her left hand, the empty one, flex as I roll the rubber onto my aching cock. She shifts her ass, pulling closer to the end of the table, splaying her knees even further apart.

I touch the tip of my cock to her entrance. She raises her head, as much as she can.

I mean to go slowly, to ease into her, but she's too ready. The ice I put inside her has melted, smoothing the way, and I drive home so fast she shudders. The tendons in her neck stand out. Her eyes strain wide.

She clutches the bandage like it's the last life preserver on a sinking ship.

"That's it, babygirl." I pull back, almost leaving the furnace between her thighs. "You can take it." I sink back in. "You're incredible, babygirl. You're amazing. You're so brave. So strong."

My pace picks up as my words carry us both away. My fingers clamp tight on her hips. Her feet stretch. Despite my size, despite the ice, despite the bonds that have to be nearing her limits, she's ready to fire in seconds.

I reach between us to find her slick clit. I wait for her to meet my gaze. I hold my body still for just a moment.

I pinch. She blinks. I slide home.

She clenches so tight around me that neither of us can move. Sunk to the hilt, I grip her hips as she bears down, as her eyes flare wide, as her jaw turns to granite. She screams into her gag, and her grip on my cock stutters loose, clenching and releasing like a second mammoth heartbeat.

I ride her for three more thrusts, my balls pulling tight. One last stroke, and I finally spill, holding her close as she clutches and drops, clutches and drops, milking me dry.

When I'm able to think again, my cheek is pressed to her belly. I can feel her breathing, fast and ragged. My thighs ripple as I stand, threatening to cramp from the strain of taking my weight.

I take care of the condom, tossing it into a stainless steel wastebasket beneath a container for sharps. Turning back to the table, I go for her gag first, deploying a pair of angled first-aid scissors to cut through the springy bandage holding it in place. I pull the cotton panties past her lips, dropping the soaked mess onto the floor.

"Babygirl," I whisper.

For a moment, she just works her jaw, rolling her lips over her teeth. I smooth her hair from her forehead. I'm a Dom. I know how to be patient.

She rallies faster than I have any right to expect. "You're a right bastard," she says, before she has to swallow. "And that was feckin' brilliant. *Sir.*"

I know she needs water, but she needs to get out of her bonds first. I scoop a melting piece of ice out of the bin at the end of the table and slip it past her lips. Then it's time for some careful work with the scissors, starting with the medical tape on her ankles, letting that stick clatter to the ground.

I take more time with her wrists, cutting away the stick that stretches her arms. Those are the muscles that have been working the longest. Even with my caution, she hisses as she finally lowers her arms to her sides. I help her, so she's spared the iron lockdown of cramps. I ease her bra off her shoulders, tossing it onto her crumpled dress.

I try to take the bandage from her hand. She doesn't need a safeword now. But she pulls it close to her chest and says, "I'm keeping this."

I let her.

When she tries to sit up, though, I settle my palms on her shoulders, holding her steady on the table. "Easy, sweetheart," I say. No more *babygirl*. Games are over now.

I help her to roll onto her side, to pull her knees toward her chest as she stretches out the taut muscles of her lower back. Only when she's steady do I cross the room for my boxers.

There's coconut water in one of the refrigerators, along with packets of the energy gel trainers squeeze down players' throats to get them back in a game. I grab the triple-berry flavor, the least disgusting of the bunch. I retrieve a white cotton blanket too—the type that can be bleached dozens of times. Helping Aeryn to sit on the side of the table, I cover her shoulders, then pull the blanket tight under her chin.

"Hold me?" she asks as I stand in front of her, taking the empty gel pack and settling the plastic lip of a water bottle against her mouth.

My heart squeezes hard enough to make me wince. "Of course," I manage to say.

I'm the luckiest man in the world, getting to sit on the table beside her. As she curls into my side, I bury my face in her hair, pulling her close, holding her tight, content just to *be*.

The treatment room is quiet, but not silent. There's the hum of the ice maker. A softer purr from the refrigerator across the room. The rasp of our breathing, easing as we both continue to recover. I'm not sure if she's still awake when there's one new sound, the faint click of both hands reaching midnight on the industrial clock mounted above the treadmill.

"Hmmm," she says, proving she's still in the realm of the living. "Merry Christmas."

I laugh. "And Merry Christmas to you. I owe you a present."

"You bought me a present—that gorgeous blue dress from Gallagher Samson. A pearl necklace too. Pearl earrings."

"And panties. But I'm sorry to say I ruined those."

"I'm not sorry."

She says it too quickly. I can make some sort of joke, tell her I'll find her something to wear in the equipment room, tell her she got what she deserved for wearing panties without lace, tell her I'll buy her replacements in Paris.

But I owe her more than that. She deserves to be taken seriously.

I try to pull away so we can have an actual discussion, but her fingers close around my wrist, holding me close. I could force the issue. I could walk across the room and pull on my jeans and my shirt, shove my feet inside my shoes.

But I let her win. I stay.

Still, I have to answer. "I'm glad you're not sorry. But what are we doing here, sweetheart? What's the plan?"

"I don't have a plan."

"You have a plane up in New York, waiting to take you back to Chicago in time for Reardon Family Christmas."

"Oh, bollocks," she says, but there isn't any heat in her voice. "I left half a message for my pilot, telling him to fetch me here."

"Half a message?"

"You walked in before I could finish. You hung up while I was leaving a voicemail."

That seems like a century ago.

"I don't want to wake him now," she says.

"He'll need to file a new flight plan."

She shakes her head. "That's not necessary."

"I'm pretty sure neither of us wants to make a midnight run to Teterboro."

"We don't have to." She shifts a hand to cover my heart. "He can take the plane back to Chicago without me. That is, if I can stay here. If you're willing to keep me."

It's impossible. It's insane. It's everything I've wanted, from the moment I first saw her standing by the bar in the Great Room. No—longer than that. This is what I've wanted since Logan Reardon first introduced me to his little sister, since she showed up at my rookie game, since I walked through the door of the house on Beach Avenue and found her primed and hot and needy and she let me be her first.

Her father won't like it. Her brothers either. I have three businesses to run—the Aces, and my real estate holdings, and Kynk. I don't have time for a woman, not a real relationship, not like the one I want with Aeryn.

No. Not *want*.

Need.

I need to be with Aeryn Reardon.

"Gage?" she asks, a shadow darkening her voice. I've taken too long to answer. Too long to tell the truth.

"Of course you can stay here," I finally answer. "I wouldn't have it any other way."

Her laughter sounds like Christmas bells. I kiss her, and she tastes like berries and daring, and that's better than any gift I've ever found beneath a tree on Christmas morning.

She's mine.

I'm hers.

It's time for a new beginning.

Thank you for reading *Sinful Mafia Santa*! I hope you enjoyed Gage and Aeryn's reunion story as much as I've enjoyed sharing it with you.

You may have noticed that *Sinful Mafia Santa* isn't as dark as other Diamond Ring romances. But that's because *you* don't know what happens on Christmas Day.

Want to find out?

Get your bonus scene by typing:

https://alixkey.com/Bonus13

into your phone or computer browser.

MORE DIAMOND RING

Or maybe you'd like to learn more about how the Diamond Ring came to exist, before all those people gathered at Radio City Music Hall? Just type:

https://alixkey.com/dring100

into your phone or computer browser.

One last thing: If you want an absolutely free full-length, totally stand-alone Diamond Ring novel, featuring a gender-switch Jack and the Beanstalk retelling and starring Irish mobster Connor Boyle, I've got you covered! Just type:

https://alixkey.com/sins

into your phone or computer browser.

THANK YOU

I can't thank you enough for choosing *Sinful Mafia Santa* from among all the dark Mafia romances out there! Without readers like you, I would never have my writing career.

You may not realize it, but *you* can be my hero. Study after study shows that the number one reason a person reads a book is because that book was recommended by a friend.

So will you tell one friend about *Sinful Mafia Santa*?

Of course, if you're dead-set on reviewing my book on Amazon and Goodreads, I won't complain! Honest reviews are hugely helpful because many advertisers require me to have a certain number of reviews before I can buy ads.

Leave a review on Amazon
Leave a review on Goodreads

Whatever you do, don't be a stranger! I look forward to hearing from you soon!

www.alixkey.com
alix@alixkey.com

ABOUT THE AUTHOR

Alix Key was born in Potomac, Maryland, where she grew up making her twin brother and all her dolls act out her favorite fairytales. When an all-grown-up Alix discovered that very real dangers lurk in the woods, she figured out how to rescue herself. She now lives outside Dover, Delaware with her own Prince Charming. When not writing dark romance, Alix serves as the Chief Operations Officer of Diamond Freeport.

You can learn more about Alix at her website, www.alixkey.com.